THREAT DETECTION

SHARON DUNN

LOVE INSPIRED SUSPENSE

INSPIRATIONAL ROMANCE

Special thanks and acknowledgment are given to Sharon Dunn for her contribution to the Pacific Northwest K-9 Unit miniseries.

LOVE INSPIRED® SUSPENSE

INSPIRATIONAL ROMANCE

ISBN-13: 978-1-335-59750-2

Recycling programs
for this product may
not exist in your area.

Threat Detection

Love Inspired
22 Adelaide St. West, 41st Floor
Toronto, Ontario M5H 4E3, Canada
www.LoveInspired.com

Printed in U.S.A.

"Been a long time, Isaac."

It felt as if she was pushing him away with each word. He was there to do a job. That's what he would focus on, not the churning turmoil he felt. "I'm sorry you were attacked. I wish we could have met again under different circumstances."

"Do you?" Again, it felt like her words were some sort of accusation.

Just focus on your job.

"I heard part of what you said to Officer Nielson. That you were high up on the volcano and someone shot at you. Did you get a look at the guy?"

She shook her head. "It doesn't make sense. What he said to me implied that I had something of his and that I should give it back."

* * *

Pacific Northwest K-9 Unit

Ever since she found the Nancy Drew books with the pink covers in her country school library, **Sharon Dunn** has loved mystery and suspense. Most of her books take place in Montana, where she lives with three nearly grown children and a hyper Border collie. She lost her beloved husband of twenty-seven years to cancer in 2014. When she isn't writing, she loves to hike surrounded by God's beauty.

Books by Sharon Dunn

Love Inspired Suspense

Fatal Vendetta
Big Sky Showdown
Hidden Away
In Too Deep
Wilderness Secrets
Mountain Captive
Undercover Threat
Alaskan Christmas Target
Undercover Mountain Pursuit
Crime Scene Cover-Up
Christmas Hostage
Montana Cold Case Conspiracy

Alaska K-9 Unit

Undercover Mission

Pacific Northwest K-9 Unit

Threat Detection

Visit the Author Profile page at LoveInspired.com for more titles.

For the invisible things of him from the creation of the world are clearly seen, being understood by the things that are made, even his eternal power and Godhead; so that they are without excuse.

—*Romans* 1:20

For my readers who keep me encouraged
and wanting to keep writing. Thank you for loving my books
and for your positive comments and reviews.

ONE

Volcanologist Aubrey Smith was grateful for the cool of the evening as she slipped out of her backpack, a nice break from the August heat. She gazed up at the focus of her research. Even though Mount St. Helens was beautiful at dusk, she had to work quickly to gather her samples and make the hefty hike back to the lab where she worked. It would be dark soon and traversing a beach of ash and then a boulder field was a challenge in daylight, so she didn't want to do it at night.

Her research in the lab at the Washington State Geological Foundation had gotten away from her, and she had not been able to leave until late in the day to get up to this spot on the volcano.

Aubrey unzipped her backpack and pulled out the sample containers. She studied the ash and pebbles on the ground. It was a specific kind of rock she was looking for that had probably only been formed in certain places when Mount St. Helens had erupted in 1980. That was the theory she was running with anyway. Volcanic rock contained crystals that grew in the magma soup underground before an eruption hurtled the rock to the surface. Studying them would shed light on the events deep in the earth that had led to the eruption.

The fading light made it hard to see. She pulled her phone from her pocket and used voice commands to turn the flashlight on. Sweeping the light over the pumice and ash, she bent down to see better.

The noise of one rock crashing against another caused her to jerk her head up. Was someone in the boulder field down below? Signs were posted to the tourists to be off the mountain before dark, and a permit was required to hike this far up the treacherous section of the mountain. Still, there was always someone who thought the rules didn't apply to them. Strange though. Because this part of the volcano required special equipment, hiking poles and gloves, and had a high level of difficulty, not many visitors chose to come this way.

She shone her light at the large black rocks below her. "Is someone down there?" Still aiming her light, she took steps toward the boulder field. "Hello, are you lost?"

The skin on her arms prickled, a fear response. Though she could not see anyone, she could feel the weight of a gaze on her.

Her heart beat a little faster as she continued to sweep the light around the rocks.

Nothing.

She told herself she was just jumpy being out here alone so close to sunset.

She turned back toward where she'd been searching for the right sample. She couldn't waste any more time.

As a child, one of her foster moms had recited a saying all the time. *We're burning daylight.* She shook her head at the memory. Bernice had been a grandmotherly type who lived on a mini farm with lots of animals. That home had given Aubrey positive memories. Not all the foster homes had.

"And I am indeed burning daylight," she said to herself, smiling at the memory of Bernice and the zoo she kept on her property.

Her hiking boots crunched on the more pebble-like ash. She moved the flashlight, spotting the type of rock she'd been looking for. She knelt and reached toward the tiny stones with a scooper.

A pinging noise made her lift her head and straighten her spine. She whirled around, glancing everywhere. Her heart raced, though she could not process what the noise was.

It sounded like a gunshot. Very close to her.

A second sound, this one closer and more explosive, confirmed her worst fear.

She was being shot at.

When she glanced toward the boulder field, a dark shadow was headed her way.

Aubrey took off running. She lifted her backpack only to have it be torn from her hands by another bullet. The man was getting closer and more accurate with each shot. In the fading light, she could not see him clearly.

She hurried to put some distance between herself and the shooter. One of her feet slipped. She righted herself. Traversing the ash beach with the poles she had brought with her was hard enough, but without that support, it was like trying to walk on ice. She gasped for breath. At this elevation, the air was very thin.

Her stumble had allowed the man to close the distance between them. There was no place to take cover. She moved as fast as she could over the precarious terrain, sliding on her behind and using her hand for support when she needed to.

Another shot came so close to her, it made her ears ring. She gasped.

Why would someone be shooting at her?

Slipping and sliding, she moved in a wide arc toward the boulder field, which would provide some cover.

Her breath came in sharp, intense jabs.

The pursuer ran steadily toward her.

Aubrey could not fathom why someone was after her. She still clutched the phone in her hand. If she could get to a hiding place, she'd be able to call for help. She knew from experience that the signal this close to the volcano was spotty at best. She needed to get closer to the wilderness trail beyond the boulder field in order to secure a signal.

She put the phone in her pocket for now.

With the pursuer nipping at her heels, she made her way to the giant lava rocks. She could hear the man's footsteps behind her as she climbed over and around various shapes of stone.

Another shot glanced off a rock just as she ducked behind it.

She kept moving. The man was so close she could hear him grunt from the effort it took to navigate this part of the mountain. She had a small advantage in that she'd been up and down this mountain so many times, she'd become an expert and knew the fastest route.

Her hands hurt from climbing. Aubrey had removed the gloves she wore on the way up and put them in her backpack. She kept going. No matter how fast she went, the man remained close. Because this part of the hike required using both hands for balance around and over the rocks, he was unable to shoot at her.

How long would this man persist in chasing her?

The rocks gave way to brush, and she could see the forest where the trail was. She sprinted toward the evergreens, bracing for another round of gunfire.

The trees loomed in front of her. If she could find a hiding place, she would be able to call for help.

Once she found the trail, she stepped across it into an area where the trees grew close together. She ran for a few minutes more then slipped behind a large trunk.

Aubrey took her phone out and stared at it, breathing a sigh of relief. She had a signal. Her finger hovered over the keypad icon as she prepared to press 911.

Footfalls very close to her caused her to freeze. Her pulse thrummed in her ears. It sounded like the man was less than ten feet from her.

Her lips quivered from intense fear.

She could hear the footsteps falling on leaves and dirt, growing softer and then louder.

Though he was close, he was still searching for her but had not pinpointed where she was.

She put her phone back in her jacket pocket, not wanting the glow from the screen to give away her location.

Light shone off to the side. He was getting closer. She drew her hands to her body and pressed against the tree trunk.

Please, God, don't let him see me.

The man shouted as he continued to swing the flashlight. "I know you're here, and I know you took it. Give it back."

What was he even talking about?

The footsteps came closer. If he shined the light this way, he'd see her for sure. Aubrey had no choice but to run. She pushed away from the tree and sprinted back toward the trail. No more gunshots were fired, yet his footsteps pounded behind her. Maybe he was out of bullets or maybe he thought it would be easier to take her out some other way.

She was in good shape from having hiked this trail

several times a week. She only hoped she was in better physical condition than the man chasing her.

As her feet pounded the trail, the man's footsteps beat like a funeral dirge behind her. Never growing louder or fading. She had to do something to shake him.

Aubrey darted off the trail into the thick of the trees. In the dim light, it was hard to see obstacles. She kept going. Then she saw her opportunity, branches leaning against a tree as if someone had started to build a lean-to. She reached out and grabbed the thickest one, whirled around and smacked the man several times, twice in the head and once in the stomach. While he was caught off guard, she kicked the back of his knees so they would buckle. He cried out and fell to the ground writhing in pain, but he wasn't unconscious. The action would only buy her seconds, but that would be enough.

She sprinted back toward where the trail was. The knowledge that she was not far from the trailhead made her run faster.

The trailhead opened up to a paved parking lot. There was only one car, which had to belong to the pursuer. It was probably locked and without keys. She ran toward where she'd secured her mountain bike and fumbled with the lock. Did she have time to do this? The lock broke free just as the man emerged from the forest and darted toward his car.

She swung her leg over the mountain bike and pushed off, pedaling frantically. She would be on the road for only a short stretch before she could get on a trail where the car could not follow.

The car roared behind her, the headlights cutting through the darkness, engulfing her. The whirring of her wheels grew more intense. She reached the place where the mountain bike trail connected with the road. Leaning hard, she veered off.

The man in the car would have to go all the way around to get to the viewing area she would come out on.

When she reached the viewing area, she stopped and pulled her phone out, then pressed 911.

"What is your emergency?"

Aubrey was so winded she could barely get the words out. "A man shot at me. I'm headed down to the Geological Foundation. He may come after me."

"Some officers are in the area. I will send them over there."

Aubrey lifted her bike up and shot across the paved viewing area toward the trail. She saw headlights in her peripheral vision. The pursuer was coming this way.

This part of the trail had tight turns and bumps. She leaned her bike and focused on not crashing, switching gears as the trail became steeper. Standing on the pedals, she caught air on the ridges. The trail opened up into the parking lot by the foundation where she worked.

Wailing sirens reached her ears. She stared up the road that the pursuer would have to take to get down here, hoping the sound of the sirens would make him stay away. Only her car remained in the employee parking lot. The foundation had closed for the day. She was alone.

She thought to shut herself in the lab for safety, but then she saw the flashing sirens of a police car. Help had arrived. Two vehicles entered the lot. A male and female officer got out of the police car, which belonged to the park police. The SUV, with a K-9 emblem on it, contained only one officer. He swung open the door and stepped out.

Aubrey thought her eyes were playing tricks on her in the evening dimness. The officer dressed in a light green uniform met her gaze, and she was sucked back in time.

She was looking at the man she'd been engaged to ten years ago, Isaac McDane.

Shaken by seeing him and everything that had just happened, she barely heard the female officer ask her a question.

"Ma'am, I'm Officer Nielson. Are you the one who phoned the police about a shooter? Can you tell me what happened?"

As he unloaded his K-9 from the kennel in the back of the SUV, Isaac's mind buzzed. The last person in the world he thought he'd ever see again was Aubrey Smith. For a moment, he doubted that it was even her until the expression on her face darkened when she saw him.

It wasn't someone who looked like Aubrey. It was her. The woman who had broken their engagement via a text when they were both only eighteen.

Freddy, a beagle trained to detect electronics, hopped down to the ground. Having his partner close made him feel like he could handle anything this job threw at him. Facing the fiancée who had dumped him, though, made him wish he hadn't been in Gifford Pinchot National Forest working a case alone. The rest of the Pacific Northwest K-9 team he was a part of were working cases in other national parks in Washington. Their bond went beyond what they did as police officers to supporting each other emotionally.

He and Freddy had just ended the day helping the Park Service Police with an investigation when he'd seen the police car and followed to see if they needed backup. He'd radioed to ask if they could use his assistance, and since it was an active shooter call, they accepted.

Aubrey gave him nervous sideways glances when he approached.

As he drew close, she turned her attention to the other two officers. He knew both of them by sight and name, having been in the area for a week.

Officer Lansbury looked at Isaac. "This woman was shot at while up at the top of the trail, and the perp chased her down the mountain."

"Is the suspect still in the area?" Freddy sat at Isaac's feet.

Aubrey nodded but didn't make eye contact. "He might still be. It takes a while to get out of the park. He was driving a dark blue sedan." She seemed rattled.

"Did you see what the man looked like?" asked Officer Lansbury.

Aubrey shook her head. "It was dark, and I was running." Her voice faltered.

Even after ten years, his instinct was to comfort her, make her feel safe.

"There is a chance we could catch him. Not much traffic at this hour," said Officer Nielson.

"He might be staying in the area at one of the hotels or lodges," Officer Lansbury said.

"If you two want to try to catch him, I can interview this woman and relay the details of the attack to you in a report," Isaac offered.

Lansbury nodded at his partner. "We better hurry. If the perp is planning on leaving the area, we don't have much time. We can put out an all-points bulletin."

Officer Nielson cupped Isaac's shoulder before running to jump in her car. "Thanks for your assistance on this."

The police car pulled away.

Isaac turned to face Aubrey. What do you say to someone after ten years and such a cruel breakup? What surprised him the most was how intensely the pain from the past rose to the surface. As if her rejection of him had just happened yesterday.

She seemed at a loss for words too.

Freddy broke the silence with a yipping look-at-me sound.

Aubrey laughed. Her face brightened as she stared down at his partner. "He's cute." Freddy wagged his tail. "And charming."

He appreciated that Freddy had found a way to break the ice.

She drew her attention back to him. "Been a long time, Isaac."

It felt as if she was pushing him away with each word. He was here to do a job. That was what he would focus on, not the churning turmoil he felt. "I'm sorry you were attacked. I wish we could have met again under different circumstances."

"Do you?" Again, it felt like her words were some sort of accusation. She was the one who had dumped him without explanation.

Just focus on your job.

"I heard part of what you said to Officer Nielson. That you were high up on the volcano, and someone shot at you. You said you didn't get a look at the guy?"

"Not really, it was dark. Everything happened so fast." She gestured toward the building by the parking lot. "If you don't mind. I need to put my bike inside."

He noticed the signage on the concrete and metal structure: Washington State Geological Foundation. "You work here?"

"Yes, I'm a volcanologist completing my PhD." Her face brightened more as she spoke about her work.

Studying volcanoes had always been Aubrey's dream. Those plans had been made when they were both eighteen. Most people didn't stick to the goals they made at that age. He certainly hadn't.

Of course, in many ways his life had not been his own when he was younger. Because he was from a prominent family, his parents had been pushing him into going to law school. He was too immature to know that that was their dream, their design on his life, not his. Besides, generations of McDanes had taken that path and been successful and happy.

Aubrey guided her bike toward the door, pulled out a key card and swiped it across the reader. He followed her inside. The building was dark. Aubrey walked to an office and pushed her bike inside.

He found himself checking out the photographs on her desk. Perhaps searching for evidence that she was dating someone. He had already noted that she didn't have a ring on her finger. It looked like mostly work-related photos. He recognized one of Aubrey with her older sister, Emily, a recent picture he guessed. He had not met Emily when he and Aubrey were dating, only seen pictures. The sisters looked alike except Aubrey was blonde and Emily's hair was light brown.

Aubrey propped her bike against the wall. After grabbing her car keys from a container on her desk, she closed the door to her office. "Do you have any more questions for me? I'd like to go home. It has been a long, hard day."

Already headed toward the door, Aubrey didn't seem to want to stand still. In addition to her having been the victim of a crime, his presence had probably stirred her up.

"I do need to ask you more questions. Can you tell me anything about the man who attacked you?"

She shook her head. "Tall, in good shape. I didn't see his face."

"Do you have any idea why someone would want to shoot at you?"

She swung the door open. She was acting like she couldn't get away from him fast enough. She shook her head. "It doesn't make sense. There is no reason someone would come after me, and if you wanted to commit a random act of violence, there are way less remote places to do that."

"So the culprit was maybe up there for a specific reason?"

Still holding the door, she turned to face him. "What he said to me implied that I had something of his and that I should give it back."

"Do you have any idea what that might be?"

She shrugged. "I was gathering samples. I didn't have anything valuable on me. All the stuff in my backpack was related to my research." She stopped for a moment. When she spoke again her voice faltered. "My backpack, my equipment, my camera, they're all still up there."

He'd seen this before with crime victims, a delayed response once the adrenaline wore off. The impact of what had happened to her was sinking in.

He stepped toward her. "You've been through a horrible attack, Aubrey. Don't discount the impact of that." He reached out and patted her upper arm.

She gazed up at him with those sparkling green eyes. "Guess I don't just brush this one off, huh?"

"It's pretty normal to be shaken by something like this," he said.

She studied him for a long moment. "Whatever made you decide to be a cop?"

"That's a long story." It was the first personal question she'd asked him. Her brisk response to being around him seemed to soften a little. "This is a pretty sweet gig though. I'm part of a team of K-9 officers who assist with investigations in the national parks in Washington State." He touched the patch on his left pocket that identified his unit.

She stepped through the door, and he and Freddy followed. Isaac stared out at the parking lot surrounded by forest.

Aubrey double-checked that the door was locked. Her blond hair fell across her face as she leaned over. She was as beautiful as he remembered.

She had just turned to face him when a gunshot disturbed the evening quiet.

TWO

Aubrey's heart pounded as Isaac pulled her down to the ground, using his body to shield her. The rough pebbles in the parking lot dug into her already raw hands. Freddy rushed over to them. Isaac rolled off her and jumped to his feet, drawing his gun.

The bullet had hit a metal sculpture by the door only inches from where she'd been standing. Her breath caught when another shot hit close to Isaac.

Freddy licked her face as if to offer comfort.

Isaac continued to scan the trees. "Run and hide behind your car. I'll cover you."

With Freddy trailing behind and his leash dragging on the ground, Isaac kept his gun pointed toward the trees, moving sideways to shield her from any bullet that might be aimed her way.

She took shelter behind the car while Isaac peered over the hood. "I've got to get to my vehicle and radio for backup. I took my shoulder radio off earlier." He looked at the dog. "Freddy, stay."

Isaac's footsteps pounded on the concrete. His SUV was at least five yards from her car. She squeezed her eyes shut and braced for the sound of another gunshot. Freddy moved in close to her. His fur brushed against her arm as if to say *I'm here for you*. She reached out to rub a velvety ear. Having the dog close helped reduce the fear that made her heart race and her body tremble.

Aubrey heard a car door open and then the sound of Isaac talking into the radio.

Still no gunshots. Maybe the shooter had realized there was too much danger of being caught and had taken off running.

By the time Isaac returned, she could hear sirens in the distance. Other police officers must have been close by.

"Lansbury and Nielson will search the road where that forest is. He must have parked somewhere." Isaac knelt close to her. Freddy took up a sitting position beside him. "Aubrey, you're coming with me," said Isaac.

"What?"

"He's come after you two times already. Until this guy is caught, you're not safe," he said.

Though she knew what he said was true, the thought of spending time with Isaac caused a tight knot in her stomach. It was clear ten years had not healed the chasm between them. Time had just numbed the hurt.

"Can't I just go back to my condo and you can arrange for a policeman to be parked outside?" Being around Isaac stirred up old pain that she thought she'd gotten past. Though he seemed to be a very good cop, she really didn't want to be reliant on him for protection.

"All that takes time to set up. What if this guy already knows where you live?"

"I don't see how this could be personal." The notion sent a shiver down her spine. "So, where do I go?"

"I've got a room at a lodge up the road. I've been staying there while I worked a case with the National Park Service. The place is not busy. I'm sure we can get you a room next door."

"Okay. I guess I have no choice." The lodge would actually be closer to work. "Can we go back to my condo and get some things? You can follow me in your vehicle. I can't leave my car here."

Isaac studied her for a long moment then looked at the trees again where the shots had come from. "Sure." He pulled his phone out. "Give me your number, and I'll text you back so you'll have mine."

Now they were exchanging phone numbers. She wanted to believe that this was just about him doing his job.

He must have picked up on her hesitation.

"For your safety, Aubrey. We need to be able to contact each other."

She recited her number.

He and Freddy made their way to the SUV. "I'll follow you, but don't let me out of your sight."

Aubrey got into her car. Another park police car pulled into the lot. The officer got out and headed toward the forest on foot, looking for the man who had shot at them. Aubrey drove toward the road. Even before she was out of the lot, she could see Isaac's car in the rearview mirror. He stayed close to her the whole time as she took the winding road that led out of Gifford Pinchot National Forest.

She turned the radio on to try to shut down the cavalcade of thoughts spinning through her head. Maybe they would catch the shooter before the night was over, and she wouldn't have to think about the past every time she looked into Isaac's eyes and saw hurt there.

She wondered if it would make a difference if he knew the whole story after all this time. They had been in love once. Or it had felt like love to her back then.

When she aged out of the foster care system, Aubrey had taken a job as a housekeeper and cook with the Mc-

Danes, a wealthy family. Their son, Isaac, had been away in Europe for the summer. When he came home, they had clicked right away. He was weeks away from going to college on the East Coast when he asked her to marry him. He didn't care about the Ivy League school; he'd go where she went.

Isaac announced their engagement at a family dinner. The response was polite but cold.

The next day Isaac's mother, Susan, had confronted her when she was alone.

Even after all these years, the words Susan spoke were like a thousand stabs to Aubrey's heart. "Isaac has a bright future ahead of him. Once he has his law degree, he could be a senator or even governor. He needs a wife who can help him make that happen."

The message was clear. Aubrey did not have the pedigree to be his wife. Marriage to her would rob him of success.

She'd cried when she sent the text.

She had broken up with him to give him the life he deserved.

After the breakup, she'd thrown herself into getting a geology degree and then grad work to forget that she had ever looked into his eyes and thought she'd found home.

His mother was right. They were a mismatch. The romance had been an illusion driven by her naivete. People like Isaac didn't marry orphan girls like Aubrey.

Honestly, until she saw him get out of that SUV, she'd thought she was long over Isaac McDane. When she looked into those blue eyes, her settled life veered toward chaos. Until she saw him, she had viewed her world as complete and fulfilling. She loved her job and the people she worked with. She had a great bunch of friends she studied the Bible with. Recently, her older sister, Emily, had come back into her life after years of estrangement.

She stared at the road in front of her and gritted her teeth.

She couldn't fix the past. The sooner she didn't have to rely on Isaac for protection, the better.

The winding road connected with the highway that led to her home, and she sped up. Traffic was light this late at night. When a sedan got between her car and Isaac's K-9 vehicle, she felt a momentary panic.

But then the car slipped into the right lane, speeding up to pass her.

Aubrey parked in front of her condo. Seconds later, Isaac pulled up behind her. She gripped the steering wheel and took several deep breaths before opening the door.

Isaac and Freddy were already waiting for her on the sidewalk. The beagle offered her a little tail wag as if to encourage her. The dog's sweetness and his ability to tune in to her emotions was endearing.

"I bet he's fun to work with," she said.

"He's all focus when we're on the job, but yes, he does have a good sense of humor," Isaac said.

"Any word from the other police officers?"

He shook his head. "They haven't caught the guy."

Her heart sank. This wasn't going to be over by tonight. If only she could just figure out what the man thought she had. She pointed at her end unit condo. "Just right over here."

With Freddy between them, they walked to her door. She twisted her key in the lock and moved to open the door.

"Wait." Isaac put his hand over hers. "I need to clear it first. Just step inside and wait by the door after Freddy and I go in."

His touch caused her heart to flutter. She shook her head at her reaction. Even after all these years. With Freddy heeling beside him, Isaac searched the living room and kitchen before heading down the hall. She turned to peer through the window at the street outside. She shuddered remembering what it felt like to be shot at and running for her life.

Isaac and Freddy came up the hall. "All clear."

"I'll just pack an overnight bag." Hopefully, that was all she would need. It was her prayer that the disruption to her life would be over tomorrow. The man who had shot her would be caught, and they would discover why he thought she had something he wanted. Then she and Isaac could part ways.

She appreciated so much that Isaac took his job seriously, but with the exception of when Freddy lightened the moment, there was a tension between them that was palpable.

A noise on the street caused her to jump. Her heart pounded. "That sounded like a gunshot."

Without hesitation, Isaac ran to Aubrey. "Get back from the window." Drawing his gun, he swung open the door and scanned up and down the quiet street, making sure the door shielded him. He stepped back inside.

Aubrey had moved deeper into the living room. Fear still clouded her face.

"I think it was just a car backfiring," he said.

"Guess I'm kind of jumpy."

He reached out and patted her arm. "Understandable." When he'd touched her hand earlier, the silkiness of her skin had reminded him of the first time they'd held hands.

He'd invited her to go for a walk with him in the evening light along the lake that bordered his parents' house.

Isaac had never put any stock in the love at first sight theory until he met Aubrey. When he'd arrived home from Europe, his dad had picked him up from SeaTac. He'd walked into the kitchen, where a woman with her blond hair in a ponytail faced the stove. She said something funny to his then twelve-year-old brother, who sat on a stool watching her cook.

His dad spoke up. "Isaac, this is Aubrey, our new live-in housekeeper and cook."

She'd turned and smiled at him. He'd never experienced anything like it before or since that moment. Her green eyes so filled with life had given a jolt to his heart.

"You must be the elusive Isaac come home after your travels." Her voice had made him think of sunsets and oceans and laughter and hot chocolate and everything that was good in the world.

Now years later as he stared at her in her living room, he realized it had all been a lie. That first time he'd opened his heart to her without hesitation. He did not care to revisit the agony she had caused him or risk it happening again.

He had a duty to see that she was safe, nothing more.

"I'll just go throw a few things in my backpack."

After she disappeared down the hall, he continued to watch the street through the window. She came out a few minutes later holding a backpack.

Before getting in the passenger seat of Isaac's SUV, Aubrey made sure her condo as well as her car were locked up.

As Isaac stared around at the other cars and people, he found himself wishing he had the backup of other members of the PNK9 team. A little extra protection for Aubrey would ensure her safety. With all the cases in the parks, the team was stretched pretty thin. He didn't want to draw resources away from where they were needed, but he missed the support of his team.

One case in particular was on the minds of everyone in the unit because it hit so close to home. Over four months ago in April, there had been a double homicide in Mount Rainier National Park, a young local couple. Their own crime scene investigator, Mara Gilmore, the ex-girlfriend of the male victim, had been seen fleeing from the murder site and had gone into hiding. His colleagues were torn over her guilt or innocence.

Isaac wiped his mind clean of concerns over ongoing cases and focused on the job at hand. He had a fleeting thought that he missed the team for another reason. It would be nice to talk to someone about how running into Aubrey had affected him.

He offered Aubrey a smile that he hoped didn't give away what was on his mind.

When he was on duty, Freddy stayed in the kennel in the custom-designed back seat. The arrangement kept the dog calm and enabled Isaac to deploy him quickly. He even had the ability to open the door remotely if needed.

Tonight, though, Isaac allowed Freddy to sit between him and Aubrey. The dog seemed to have a comforting effect on her. They drove in the darkness back to the national forest, first on the highway and then on the road that led to the lodge.

Because he'd promised a write-up for the other officers on what had happened to Aubrey and any details that might help the investigation, he thought he could use the time to extract as much information from her as he could.

Aubrey petted Freddy's head. She seemed calmer, as if the shock of the attack had worn off. Forgotten details might come back to her.

"Do you have any theories why someone would shoot at you or any ideas about what he wanted from you?"

"The only valuable thing I had with me was my camera. That's certainly not worth killing for. And that is still up there." She laced her fingers together and then stared out the front window. "I just don't get it."

"What were you doing up there that late in the day?"

"Gathering samples of rock and ash."

"The place where you were shot at, is it busy during the day? Maybe somebody dropped something valuable and came back for it."

"So valuable it was worth shooting at me to get it?"

"I know it seems like an extreme reaction, but we don't know what he was up there for. Is it a place where someone could have dropped something important or even stowed it and come back for it?" Isaac kept his eyes on the road as he talked.

"No, it's the part of the volcano with the least amount of tourist traffic because it's so inaccessible compared to the other parts of the mountain. No research has been done there in years. I just recently put in a request to gather samples there based on a theory I have."

"Do you feel comfortable trying to remember the details of what happened?"

"If it will help catch this guy," she said.

"Close your eyes and try to envision exactly what you did right before the first shot was fired."

"I put my backpack on the ground and pulled my collection containers out. It was starting to get dark, so I grabbed my phone to use its flashlight. I was looking for rock with a specific coloration." She stopped for a moment, opening her eyes when he slowed down to turn.

"Keep going. What did you do next?"

"I found the kind of rock I was looking for, so I leaned

over to gather a sample…that's when the first shot was fired."

"It sounds like the guy thought you picked up the item he came up there to get."

"Yes, now that I think about it, it does. My back was to him when I leaned over. He probably didn't see that I had a container in my hand."

"So, whatever he was looking for is still up there, but he thinks you have it. We need to go back to the spot where you were," said Isaac.

"I can do that in the morning once I check in at work. I have to retrieve my gear I left up there anyway."

"Good. We have a plan." When he pulled up to the lodge, most of the room windows were dark. The lights in the office glowed. "We'll need to get up there as early as possible."

"Should we go see if they have a room for me?" She pushed open the door.

"Wait. There is a foldout couch in my room. I'll sleep on it and you can have the bed."

The look on her face told him she was not comfortable with being in such close quarters with him. "Why? You said you thought there would be a room for me."

He let out a breath. "I didn't want to alarm you. But there was a car following us most of the way here. When I turned off into the lodge parking lot, it went down the road. It could be nothing, but we can't take any chances."

Her eyes grew wide, revealing that the fear had returned. "Okay, if that is how it has to be."

Why did it hurt that she didn't want to be around him? If only the intense emotions of the past were washed clean from his mind and heart, he would be able to do his job and protect her.

He handed her his key card. "I'm in room 7. I chose the

first floor so I can get out easily for Freddy to do his business, which I have to take care of right now. If you want to go inside, I'll be there in just a minute."

She took the key card from him. While he commanded Freddy to dismount, he stayed close to make sure she was safely inside. He led Freddy to a grassy area designated for pets.

His phone rang. His colleague, fellow PNK9 officer Ruby Orton, one of his good friends on the team, was calling. Ruby had been with the unit for four years. She worked search and rescue with a sweet black Lab named Pepper.

"Hey, Ruby," he said. "How's life in Mount Rainier National Park?"

"I'm actually on my way to meet Eli for dinner," she said. Isaac pictured Eli Ballard, the new man in Ruby's life. They'd met on the team's biggest case, since Eli was the business partner of Stacey Stark, the female victim who'd been shot to death in the park along with her boyfriend. Stacey and Eli were equal owners of the three Stark Lodges, which were located very close to national parks in Washington State.

"On one hand, I feel a little guilty having a nice Italian dinner on a date while all my teammates are working so hard on their cases. But since I often talk to Eli about Stacey and the lodges and who might have wanted to harm her and Jonas Digby, I feel justified in having a love life. What do you think?"

Isaac laughed. "I think you're totally justified, Ruby. You deserve all the happiness in the world." He meant every word. He'd once thought he'd found happiness and love—with Aubrey—but it had all been a lie. Isaac was naturally a little suspicious of Eli Ballard, since he'd briefly been on the short list of suspects given his connection to the victims in the Mount Rainier National Park murders. But Eli had a solid alibi and had been very helpful to all the PNK9 officers who'd dealt with him.

"Are you on your way back home?" Ruby asked.

Isaac lived near Mount Rainier, the park to which he was assigned. "Actually, no. I'm on a case here." He briefly told her about it. Including that he and Aubrey had been involved when they were very young.

"Wow," she said. "I'm here if you need to talk, Isaac."

"I'll keep that in mind," said Isaac.

While he appreciated Ruby's support, talking about Aubrey blew his focus. He had to be all about the case and keeping her safe until they figured out who was after her and why. He said his goodbyes to Ruby and disconnected the call.

He felt a tightening in his chest as he surveyed the road where the other car had driven past. He prayed that it was just someone out for a late-night drive and that Aubrey would be safe from another attack tonight.

THREE

Morning light shining through the window caused Aubrey to open her eyes. She sat up, grateful to have had a night's sleep without disruption. A blanket lay on the couch where Isaac had slept. He hadn't even bothered to sleep on the foldout bed.

She'd fallen asleep to the sound of him working on a laptop; she assumed it was his report on the attack on her. No noise came from the bathroom. She wondered where Isaac had gone.

Fear crept in at the thought of being alone in the room after what Isaac had said about the car that had followed them. His choice to bring her here had been sound. She wouldn't have been safe at her condo alone. As uncomfortable as things were between them, she was grateful for Isaac's protection.

She pulled the covers off. She'd slept in her clothes so she'd feel ready to pop out of bed at a moment's notice if need be. Plus the underlying tension between her and Isaac made her not want to be in close proximity to him in her pajamas. Neither of them was prone to anger. But a smoldering strain between them made it feel like a fight could erupt at any time. As long as they didn't talk about the past, maybe she could make the best of the time she had to be around him.

She closed her eyes and prayed.

Lord, just get me through this.

A thumping noise drew her attention to Freddy, who gazed up at her from the side of the bed with expressive brown eyes. The floppy ears only added to his appeal.

"Hey there. Glad you stuck around to watch over me," she said.

She reached down to give her new friend some affection. She had never had a pet as a child. Her father had died when she was five, and she'd lost her mother months after she was born. Some of the foster homes she'd been in had family pets, but never an animal that was bonded to her.

She got down on the carpet to rub Freddy's ears. "You are a sweetie."

The door burst open, and Isaac stepped inside holding two wrapped packages. "I see my partner is working his charm on you."

She stroked Freddy's head, which made him nuzzle her hand. "He's a good guy."

He lifted the packages. "I talked the kitchen into making us some breakfast burritos. We can eat them on the way to the trailhead that leads up to where you were."

"We need to stop at the foundation first. I have to let my boss know what happened and that I won't be available to help out in the lab or with programs we do for the public."

"Will it take long? I think time is of the essence that we get to where the shooting occurred quickly. I know you said it was low traffic area, but I don't want it disturbed before I gather evidence," Isaac said.

"It's a pretty hefty hike. You'll need equipment that we have at the foundation. At the very least, you'll need water for you and this little guy."

"I have a pack in the vehicle. A lot of the work my unit does takes me into the back country, so we are prepared for that contingency."

"You and your colleagues are federal officers working for the national parks?" Aubrey asked.

"Yes, we're based out of Olympia. We're brought in anytime the park service needs specialized help with their cases, including K-9s. All the dogs have different specialties—search and rescue, suspect apprehension, almost anything you could think of."

"I know I love that my job lets me be so close to nature. It must be a fun job for you too?" Love for the outdoors had been one of the things they had had in common.

"It's worthwhile. I like that it feels like I am making a difference."

"Not where you thought your life was going though?" Almost as soon as she asked the question, she regretted it. Anything that brought up their past held the danger of conflict between them.

The darkening of his expression told her she had been right. "After my parents died, I had to reassess my life."

His words were laden with vulnerability. "I saw the newspaper story about the plane crash. I am truly sorry."

His tone grew soft. "Now we both know the pain of losing parents."

She nodded, looking into the depth of his blue eyes and knowing that words would cheapen the moment of connection between them.

Freddy let out a whimper and brushed against her hand. The dog was so tuned in to the emotions in the room. She knelt on the floor and rested her forehead against the top of Freddy's head. "This guy has won my heart."

Isaac chuckled. "Let's get going. I don't want to be hiking in the heat of the day."

Within minutes, they were in the SUV and headed toward the foundation. When they arrived, five cars were in the employee parking lot.

She released her seat belt. "I'll just be a minute. I need to quickly talk to my boss and then grab a water bottle and some hiking gear. Do you have gloves and poles?"

He shook his head. "How strenuous is this hike?"

"It's not for the faint of heart. I'll grab some for you too." She drew her attention to the foundation entrance. Seeing the metal sculpture with the bullet hole in it made her shudder.

He clicked out of his seat belt as well. "I'll come with you."

She swung open the door, and they stepped inside. The second she saw three of her colleagues in a huddle, she knew something was wrong. One of them, Duncan LaRoy, noticed Aubrey and walked toward her. Though Duncan was not her direct supervisor, he often acted like it. He was always quick to point out that he had a PhD, and she was still working on hers. Plus Duncan had been at the foundation longer than anyone else.

Duncan looked at Isaac. "That was quick."

"What do you mean?" Isaac shook his head, confused. He looked behind him as if Duncan might be addressing someone else.

"Aren't you the police officer we called?"

Isaac shook his head.

Aubrey's breath caught in her throat as fear rose to the surface. "Duncan, what are you talking about?"

"We think there may have been a break-in," Duncan said.

"Why? Was something missing?"

"Not that we could tell." Duncan pointed at one of the other scientists. "Christopher noticed a smear on the glass looking in on the old simulation lab downstairs. You know how clean he likes things to be kept. And a box sitting outside of a storage room in the basement looked like it had been kicked out of alignment."

"Any one of us could have done that," said Aubrey. Christopher was a brilliant scientist who had a high need for order and things being tidy. He would be the one to notice if anything was amiss, but none of this sounded like a crime so far.

"Were there any signs of a break-in?" Isaac asked.

"Not on the exterior door—" Duncan shook his head "—but when we looked at the parking lot security camera footage, there was someone in the lot at midnight three nights ago. He or she was wearing a hoodie. Right after that, the camera stopped working. We don't know why. I already put in an order to get it fixed." Duncan turned toward Aubrey. "It wasn't you, was it?"

Aubrey didn't like the level of accusation in Duncan's voice. "No. Why would I be skulking through the parking lot at that hour?"

"It wasn't any of us either," Duncan said. "That's why we called the police. Maybe that smear on the glass will have a print on it."

The two officers who had assisted Aubrey last night stepped into the reception area of the foundation. Duncan excused himself and walked over to address Officers Lansbury and Nielson.

The news left Aubrey's mind reeling. She wanted to believe that there hadn't even been a break-in. And if there was, it wasn't connected to what had happened to her on Mount St. Helens. She wasn't about to talk to Duncan about being shot at.

Instead, she made her way to her direct supervisor's office. Leandra Ware was a woman in her early sixties who could still keep up with someone half her age when they were in the field doing research. Though her job required her to spend more time in front of a computer than outdoors, she still dressed in boots and clothes designed for hiking.

Leandra greeted Aubrey with a broad smile.

Aubrey explained about the attack the night before at the research site and in the employee parking lot.

Leandra set her coffee cup down. "That sounds very serious."

"With your permission, I need to go back up there where it happened. A police officer has agreed to go with me."

Leandra touched her steel-gray bun. "After what Duncan said he saw on that tape, this is very concerning. Certainly, if you need to head back up there, go ahead."

Aubrey grabbed two sets of hiking poles, gloves and a spare backpack from the equipment room. When she returned to the reception area, Isaac was conversing with the police officers.

He turned to face her. "Ready?"

She nodded. The desk where her sister, Emily, was supposed to be working was empty. Emily was a year older than Aubrey. Their relationship had been strained since Emily's teen years when she had started to run with the wrong sort of people. Aubrey and her sister had sometimes been together when they were in foster care, but often that was not possible. About a month ago, Emily had gotten in touch wanting to turn her life around. Aubrey had put in a good word for her to get a job doing administrative work for the foundation. It felt like their relationship was on the mend.

The receptionist, Mary, looked up from her computer.

"Are you looking for Emily? She came in but then she left abruptly."

Aubrey's stomach twisted into a knot. "Did she say why?"

"Just that she was feeling under the weather," said Mary.

She hoped that was all that was going on with her sister. She clenched her jaw. Why did her mind always jump to the worst-case scenario where her sister was concerned?

After Isaac ushered her outside and they got into his SUV, she felt herself becoming even more anxious. What did it mean if the break-in was connected to what happened to her? Her office hadn't been ransacked. The person in the hoodie had been here three nights ago. The attack on her had happened last night.

"Do the officers know about the shooter taking another shot at me outside the foundation?"

"Yes, it was all in my report, and I got them up to speed while they were there dealing with the break-in," Isaac said.

"If there was no sign of a break-in, maybe the person on the tape was just somebody running through the lot, even though I agree, it looks suspicious. Duncan said they didn't know why the camera malfunctioned. A raccoon could have decided he liked it."

"Even if that smear yields a fingerprint, it won't mean there wasn't a crime if it belongs to someone who works here." Isaac kept his eyes on the road while he talked.

"I don't understand what you're implying," said Aubrey.

"Usually, when there is no sign of a break-in, it means it was an inside job. Someone who had a key to the place," he said.

"We don't even know if there was a break-in. The stuff

that Christopher noticed doesn't mean anything. Nothing was stolen or even sabotaged…far as we know." Aubrey was surprised at how emotional she'd become. Everyone that worked there including Emily had a key to get into the building.

"Right, we don't know anything yet." His voice was calm and reassuring. "What matters is evidence. I'd like to get a look at the camera footage of the person in the hoodie. Body language says a lot about intent."

He pulled into the lot where the trailhead was. A brown-and-tan Forest Service sign identified the place as the Gifford Pinchot National Forest, Climber's Bivouac.

They had a long day ahead of them. She hoped by the end of it, this whole thing would be resolved.

As she slipped her backpack over her shoulders and grabbed the other equipment, she had a feeling that despite her wish, the trouble was only beginning.

Isaac got Freddy out of his kennel and poured him some water from the supply pack he always had with him The pack held a collapsible dish that he could put the water in. Freddy had eaten before they left the lodge.

Several other cars were at the trailhead parking lot. A young couple headed toward the trees.

"Does it get busy here?"

"Yes, especially this time of year. August is the height of tourist season. Once the trail splits off to the harder to access area, we are not likely to see many people. You need a permit to go through the boulder field to the summit."

Aubrey's agitation over what might have happened at the foundation was understandable, but he wondered if there wasn't something deeper going on. She seemed to get more upset when she asked the receptionist about her sister, Emily.

Isaac had never met Emily. Only seen pictures of her. At the time they were dating, Aubrey was estranged from her sister and had shared that her sister had chosen to be with people who were a bad influence. Even then, he had heard the pain that the distance between Aubrey and her only sibling caused.

They headed toward the trailhead marker. Another car came and parked in the lot as they stepped onto the hiking path. Aubrey kept up an intense pace. Even though it was August, the tree canopy and the early morning hour meant it was cool for now.

Other hikers either walking down or passing them did a double take when they saw Isaac's uniform and Freddy. Only one hiker asked if there had been a crime committed. Isaac offered a vague answer.

The trees thinned, and he could see the boulder field up ahead. "Wow."

"I know—pretty incredible. All that lava rock got displaced during the eruption over forty years ago. Huge landslides for miles. Acres of trees knocked down. The whole Toutle River valley was affected by the lahar, a deposit of debris and ash left by the landslide from the eruption. Spirit Lake got filled with logs."

A tone of admiration filled her voice. The same way a person who loves art talks about a painting. Her passion about volcanos had been one of the things that he had loved about her.

"Nature is amazing," said Isaac.

"And powerful." Aubrey shook her head. "I think as a child when I saw the beauty and the power of nature, I knew that there was a God."

"And now you get to be around it every day," he said.

Aubrey nodded and stopped to put her gloves on. "We

can mostly go around the rocks, but there are a few steep parts. How will Freddy handle that?"

"Like a trooper." Isaac pulled his gloves out as well. "He's never shown hesitation about following me into all kinds of situations. If it gets too precarious, I have a carrier I can put him in, one of the advantages of working with a smaller dog. We need to be ready for anything, including the shooter coming after you again."

Aubrey's expression grew serious as she nodded. "I am well aware of that."

The sun grew more intense as they hiked and climbed through the boulder field. Only once did he have to carry Freddy. When the boulder field gave way to pumice, ash and a steep vertical climb, Aubrey lengthened the poles she'd hooked onto her belt.

She planted her poles and turned to face him. The sun brought out the golden highlights in her blond hair. "The pumice and ash can be slippery. The best way to traverse this is to treat it like you are on cross-country skis, slide, stop, slide, stop."

"I'll follow you," he said.

He looked down at Freddy, who tilted his head as if to say *Are you kidding me?*

The little dog proved himself to be more sure-footed than Isaac, who felt like he was sliding on ice.

They hiked until the sun was a quarter way above the horizon. Aubrey turned to face him. "Doing okay?"

While he was sweating and out of breath, she just looked dewy. The hike seemed to energize her and lift her mood.

"I'll survive," he said.

"Don't feel bad about being out of breath. We'll climb over a thousand feet in a short time. Plus the air is thinner up here."

He managed to nod, unable to form words between gasps. Aubrey was completely in her element with this hike. It made her seem even more beautiful.

He kept his focus on her bobbing blond ponytail as they climbed. She slowed down and then stopped. He came up beside her.

She pointed with her pole. "That's where it happened."

The sun caused a shimmering mirage effect as he stared out at a backpack and other items he couldn't identify at this distance. He had evidence bags with him and flag markers. Maybe he could find some shell casings and take some pictures with his phone. It would be quite an undertaking to get a full crime scene team up here. He wasn't sure if the park service could spare the manpower. The PNK9 unit had their own crime scene investigators, but with their rookie, Mara, in hiding and her boss, Bartholomew, spread thin, Isaac wouldn't bother the chief with the request. Besides, headquarters was hours away from Mount St. Helens.

"Do you feel like you could show me what happened, where you were when he shot at you?"

Her face blanched as she stared ahead, but she nodded and stepped forward. "I was over there by where I dropped my sample collection container." She kept walking and picked a container up off the ground and mimed her actions as she described them. "It was starting to get dark. I had the flashlight out on my phone so I could see the coloring of the rock sample I was looking for."

Isaac stepped toward her with Freddy heeling beside him.

Aubrey kept talking as she turned her back to them. "When I found the rock I was looking for, I knelt down."

Isaac and Freddy were only a few feet from her.

She turned back around and pointed down to where

the boulder field met the ash beach. "I think the first shot came from there."

He scanned the area for shell casings. The sun should reflect off the metal.

Freddy whimpered and shifted his weight side to side.

"What is it, big guy?"

"Can he find shell casings?"

"It's not his specialty. He's trained to sniff out electronics, anything from cell phones to SD cards."

Something had Freddy stirred up. Isaac gave the command for Freddy to do his thing. The dog put his nose to the ground, moving back and forth at first and then in smaller and smaller circles. He sat down, which was his signal that he had alerted on something.

Both Isaac and Aubrey stepped closer to where Freddy was.

"There." Aubrey pointed.

Isaac focused on a tiny patch of blue not far from Freddy's paw. It was nearly concealed by the gray ash.

After rewarding Freddy with a treat, he stepped closer and put on evidence gloves and picked it up—a thumb drive.

"That has to be what that shooter came up here for," she said.

Isaac glanced around half expecting to see the shooter.

"How did Freddy find it so quickly?"

"There is a chemical on all circuit boards that he can smell. It's a kind of oxide. Too hard to pronounce. We just call it TPPO for short."

Aubrey reached down to pat Freddy's head. "Good boy."

Isaac held up the thumb drive. "I wonder what is on this that is worth killing for to get it back?"

FOUR

It was late afternoon by the time Aubrey and Isaac made it back to the trailhead. She looked at her watch. Three o'clock. She could still get in some hours at work. The team was going to do some scaled simulations in the new lab upstairs.

Though she was used to the hike, having to revisit where she'd nearly been killed was traumatizing and had left her exhausted. Maybe she wouldn't go back to work.

They walked over to Isaac's PNK9 vehicle. There were fewer cars in the lot than there had been in the morning. None of the cars looked like the shooter's but that didn't mean he couldn't still be around.

She decided that she didn't have the energy to go back into the foundation. Finding out what was on the thumb drive seemed more important. "Can I be with you when you look at that thumb drive?"

"Sure. Why don't we grab a bite and head back to the lodge?" said Isaac.

Her stomach growled at the mention of food. She had only eaten an energy bar while they were hiking. "Okay."

After securing Freddy in the back seat, Isaac got behind the wheel. "There was a hamburger food truck I ate at when I was helping out the Forest Service. How does that sound?"

"I know which one you're talking about. They have decent food and they're quick." After all that had happened, she found herself not wanting to be out in the open. She'd feel safer once they were in the room at the lodge with the door locked.

They picked up their burgers and fries and drove to the lodge. Isaac pulled up close to the door of the room where they were staying. He handed her the key card. She already held both to-go containers.

"If you could open the door, I have to get Freddy out."

She'd placed the key card on top of the to-go containers in order to have a free hand to open the vehicle's door. She walked over to the room. As she reached for the key, the door burst open and a man crashed into her. The food flew in the air, and she landed on her bottom. The man who had knocked her down took off running toward the trees that surrounded the lodge. Freddy and Isaac were right behind him.

Isaac shouted at her as he ran by. "Get inside. Lock it."

Aubrey stared at the fries and burgers scattered all over the ground. Shaking, she picked up the key card and pushed herself to her feet. She stumbled toward the open door.

What she saw inside made her knees buckle. She reached out for the door frame for support. The drawers were open; everything had been emptied out of her overnight bag and Isaac's suitcase.

She stepped inside, turned the dead bolt and collapsed in a chair, trying to slow her pounding heart with deep breaths. No good. Her body felt like it was being shaken from the inside.

When that didn't work, and she thought she might faint, she leaned over and put her face between her knees. This shooter seemed to find her no matter where she was.

Oh God, please give me strength.

After a minute or so, she raised her head and felt calmer. She noticed that Isaac's laptop was not where he'd left it on the foldout couch. The screen glowed from where it had been placed on the table by the window.

She rose to her feet and walked across the room. Once he didn't find a thumb drive, the shooter must have been looking for downloaded files.

She tensed and rubbed her arms.

The culprit had figured out which room she was in at the lodge. As long as he was on the loose, there was no safe place for her.

She only hoped that Isaac and Freddy were able to catch him.

With Freddy taking up the lead, Isaac chased after the shooter who had been in the room. No doubt searching for the thumb drive he and Aubrey had just found. The man quickly left the trail and wove through the trees. Freddy padded along at a brisk pace. The beagle was not trained to track, but he had good instincts.

Though his legs were fatigued from the all-day hike, Isaac pulled his gun and moved in the general direction he'd last seen the culprit running.

He called for backup on his radio, giving his location.

A shot was fired in Isaac's direction. Adrenaline flooded his body as he slipped behind a tree and pressed his back against the trunk. Freddy brushed against his calf, pushing close to Isaac. The beagle was not fazed by the gunfire.

This guy was playing offense, trying to take Isaac out instead of just escape. The conversation on the radio must have given away his position.

Backup was on the way, but he didn't think he could wait for them if he had hopes of taking the culprit in.

He wanted the shooter in custody to end the threat to Aubrey's life and get some answers.

With his weapon drawn, he rolled along the tree trunk, scanning the forest for signs of another person. Tuning his ears to the sounds around him, he listened for something distinctly human. He glanced down at Freddy to see if he gave a sign of noticing anything. The beagle lifted his head to sniff the air.

Isaac took a step away from the tree. Not even a light breeze rustling the branches disturbed the heavy silence. His heart drummed in his ears.

Though Freddy was a very vocal dog, he seemed to understand the need to be quiet.

Isaac held the gun at a ready position with his finger across the trigger guard as he took a step out into an open area. Still nothing. The shooter must have crept away.

Isaac moved faster in the direction the shot had come from. He heard a car start-up. He sprinted toward the noise, stepping out onto a viewing area just in time to see a car disappear around a curve. Other than its proximity to the lodge, he had no idea what road the shooter was on or where he might be going.

He radioed backup. "Perp escaping in a dark sedan near the lodge. By my estimation he is headed south."

But was he?

Fear gripped Isaac. What if he was going back to the lodge to harm Aubrey? The shooter knew she was alone. Isaac hurried back through the trees while Freddy kept pace with him. He knocked on the door to his room. "Aubrey, it's me."

He heard the dead bolt slide and she opened the door.

"You're okay." He reached out to hug her but caught himself.

"Yes." She stepped aside so he could enter the room.

It didn't surprise him that the place had been tossed. The perp seemed to be operating on the premise that Aubrey had found the thumb drive last night. His presence, the uniform and the PNK9 vehicle would have indicated to the shooter that law enforcement was onto him. Yet, he seemed willing to take big risks to get what he was looking for.

"Did you get a look at the guy?"

She shook her head. "It happened so fast. Same build as the man who came after me at the volcano."

Isaac pulled the thumb drive from the zippered pocket where he'd put it. "Why don't we straighten this place up and see what is on this?"

After they had put away everything that had been pulled out and messed with, Isaac walked over to his laptop and stuck the thumb drive in, watching the screen and holding his breath. Maybe now they would get some answers.

FIVE

Aubrey leaned close to Isaac as a series of icons popped up on the screen, five folders containing JPEGs.

Isaac clicked on the first one. A man in a suit on a downtown street. The same man photographed from a distance as he ran on a jogging path. Photos of a car with the license plate taken in a close-up shot. He clicked on another file. The first image was of a different man sitting at a coffee shop with a laptop. The picture was taken from outside through the window. The man had long stringy hair and was dressed in oversize clothes. Another photo was of the same unkempt man entering an apartment building. Again, there was a close-up shot of the apartment building number and then a mailbox that said Apt 515.

Another folder revealed a man with a beard going into a posh-looking hotel. Even in the photos he had an over-powering presence. In every shot, he had the same two men beside him. The bulge in their jackets indicated they had guns and were probably bodyguards.

"I know that hotel. Not far from here, in Longview where I live. Very expensive," Aubrey said.

"These look like surveillance photos," Isaac said. He clicked on a fourth folder. "A lot of them are taken from a distance with a telephoto lens."

Aubrey gasped as the first image came up. "That's my sister outside her apartment."

"That's Emily?"

Isaac filed through the remaining images: Emily at a park, Emily at the foundation, Emily's car. Aubrey found it hard to take in a deep breath. What had her sister gotten herself mixed up in?

"Any idea of why your sister would be on here?" He opened the last folder, which revealed similar images of a different man. One of the images was of the man headed into a climbing facility. Another showed a cabin with a close-up of the address on the mailbox.

Aubrey rose to her feet and paced. "Why would someone collect pictures like that?"

"Hard to say," Isaac said. "The one thing I do know is this is way bigger than I first thought. I'm going to see if I can get a couple of my colleagues to help me, starting with our tech expert, Jasmin. It should be easy enough to match the pictures that have addresses to a name, then we have to figure out what the connection between these five people is."

Aubrey's thoughts raced as Isaac tapped the keyboard of his laptop. Was Emily in some kind of danger? She grabbed the phone and dialed Emily's number. After five rings it went to voice mail. She hung up without leaving a message. "Emily's not picking up."

He looked up from his typing for a second. "If she's actually sick as she told the receptionist, she might be asleep and have the phone turned off."

She sent a text to her sister. R u ok? Sometimes Emily just didn't want to talk. The question was a shorthand way of relaying a message that they had developed when they were teenagers in the same foster home. Emily had been getting into a lot of trouble back then. It was the quickest way for Aubrey to know that her sister was alive without prying or requiring an explanation.

Still gripping the phone, she collapsed onto the bed. After licking her hand, Freddy jumped up on the bed beside her, pressing close to her leg and then resting his head on her thigh. Expressive brown eyes gazed up at her as she listened to Isaac's phone call.

"Jasmin, how are things on your end?" He quickly brought her up to speed on his case. "Look, I've just downloaded some folders containing photographs." He tapped the keyboard. "I'm sending them to you right now. It would be great if we could get some names attached to these pictures. We already know the identity of the woman. Her name is Emily Smith. Her sister is the one who was shot at last night. Emily also works at the foundation."

Aubrey could hear a woman talking on the other end of the line though she could not discern what was being said.

"Sure, give me a call as soon as you know something." He looked at his watch. "Oh, I didn't realize it was so late. Sounds like you got a lot on your plate. I'll wait to hear from you in the morning."

He hung up and stared at the computer screen for a long moment before pulling the thumb drive out and putting it back in the zippered pocket of his jacket. "This stays with me at all times until I can get it turned in to evidence."

Her phone dinged, indicating she had a text. Emily's name came on the screen.

Doing Ok. Don't worry about me.

She took in a breath. Emily was safe but did not want to share more information. After so many years of slipping in and out of each other's lives, her relationship with her sister was fragile. She didn't want to jeopardize what they had begun to rebuild together by making accusations or even asking questions. Emily was her only family. She wanted her sister in her life.

Her stomach growled. "What are we going to do since our dinner is scattered all over the courtyard?"

"The lodge has a little restaurant here, limited menu, but it's better than going hungry." He must have picked up on how preoccupied she was about her sister. "Jasmin is a whiz at working through information. We should have some answers in the morning."

She nodded.

"We'll just have to hang tight." He rose to his feet and cupped her shoulder. "Let's go get something to eat."

Leaving Freddy alone in the room with his dinner, they stepped outside where the sky was growing dark. A few stars twinkled in the sky.

Isaac's gaze moved around the courtyard and parking lot as if he was expecting another attack. She edged a little closer to him as they entered the restaurant.

Only two of the five tables were occupied. One with an older couple and the other with a man who looked to be in his early twenties. His deep tan indicated he spent a great deal of time outside. He could be on one of the fire crews that was in the park every summer or maybe he was a hiker.

"Why don't we get some sandwiches to go?" Isaac said as he studied the menu that was written on a chalkboard behind the counter.

The suggestion made it clear that Isaac didn't want to be out in the open for long.

A middle-aged lady in an apron emerged from a back room. "What can I get you for?"

"Do you have anything that is quick that we can take back to our room?"

"How do club sandwiches, chips and a drink sound to you?"

Aubrey was so hungry she could eat her shoe at this point. "That would be great."

"Give me just a few minutes." The woman disappeared through the swinging doors.

While they waited, Isaac's radio fizzed, and a female voice came on the line. "Officer Nielson here. Just wanted to let you know we did not locate the car you described on any of the roads around the lodge. Suspect is still at large."

The bad news made Aubrey's heart beat a little faster. The shooter was still out there.

Once they got their food, they headed back to the ground floor room at the lodge. Isaac handed her the to-go containers so his hands would be free. She knew he was thinking about the possibility of the man taking another shot at her.

They stood outside the door of the room.

"Look," said Isaac. "I'm going to see if we can get one of the suites on the second floor. You're just too vulnerable on the ground floor. That way we'll both have a room. This thing is not going to be over anytime soon. I'm going to have to pull in some more PNK9 officers to help me get it resolved."

The realization that her life would not go back to normal quickly was frustrating. And now she was going to have to spend more time with Isaac. "If that is what we have to do." The one consolation was that it was clear that Isaac was very good at his job.

"Why don't you go inside and wait with Freddy? I'll

look into getting us moved." Isaac swiped the key card and opened the door for her.

Freddy greeted her enthusiastically, his ears flopping around as he ran toward her. She stepped inside and closed the door. She slid the dead bolt in place and sat down.

Aubrey felt like the walls were closing in on her.

The man who had tried to kill her was still out there. It was just a matter of time before he came after her again.

Once settled in the new suite on the second floor, they sat at the table to eat their sandwiches. Isaac's mind was racing with the calls he needed to make. The first one would be to his boss, Chief Donovan Fanelli, to see how many resources they could allocate to this case. The team was assigned to the state's three national parks—Mount Rainier, Olympic and North Cascades—but since the attack on Aubrey occurred in a national forest park, he was sure the chief would be open to sending an officer or two. And hopefully, Jasmin would be able to connect the dots between the five people whose photos were on that thumb drive.

Aubrey was going to need protection while she was at work. Would it be worth it to see if they could get a crime scene team up to where the shooting had taken place? The crime scene personnel with the state park would normally be utilized since the attack had happened under their jurisdiction. He knew from having helped out the park police that they were stretched thin this time of year.

Aubrey took a bite of her sandwich and nibbled on some chips. "You're being awful quiet."

"Just trying to come up with a plan for what has become a full-scale investigation," he said.

"Do you like your job?"

"I like knowing I'm helping people," said Isaac. "The rest of the team I work with are great. Really, it's the best part in some ways."

Her gaze flickered around the room. "I remember you talking about going into politics."

He knew any talk about the past was the equivalent of walking into a minefield. "My plans changed."

"What made you want to be a police officer and work with a dog?"

That was a safe enough question. "I was doing volunteer work with at-risk kids. We had a K-9 officer as a guest speaker. When I saw how the officer and his partner worked together, something clicked for me."

"Maybe it was your mom and dad more so than you who thought law school was the way to go." She put down her half-eaten sandwich.

She seemed to be hinting at something, but again, keeping the peace so he could provide protection seemed like the highest priority right now. "Plans change. You're the only person I've met who knew what she wanted to be from an early age and carried it out."

"I can't imagine doing anything else. I would have done research at any volcano. I like that it was the one my father took me to see before he died."

Before Aubrey's father passed away, he'd taken her and her sister on a trip to the volcano. She carried the memory of having visited Mount St. Helens with her like most people wore a locket with a picture in it.

"I admire what you've accomplished," he said. "It couldn't have been easy."

As she met his gaze, something in her expression softened. "Thank you. It was quite a challenge to get this far, but I would not have traded a minute of it."

The moment that had the potential to become explosive had instead made him feel closer to her. While he had always felt the weight of expectation with his family from generations of successful bankers and lawyers, she had had the opposite. Given her background, no one had thought Aubrey Smith would make something of herself. But he had seen it from the moment he'd met her. That spine of steel determination and the clear vision she had for her future.

She pushed her chair back from the table. "I can't eat any more. I'm exhausted. I think I will just shower and go to sleep."

"I don't blame you," he said.

He watched as she disappeared into one of the bedrooms and closed the door behind her.

Carrying his sandwich with him, he rose to his feet and stared out the window at the courtyard below. One of the two streetlamps was not working, leaving the area shrouded in darkness. The window allowed him a view of the road that connected to the lodge parking lot. If someone pulled in, he would see them.

He took the last few bites of his sandwich.

Freddy came and sat beside him. "One more potty run, huh, buddy?"

He put Freddy's leash on, double-checked that the door was locked behind him and headed down the exterior stairs so Freddy could go to the bathroom. On his way back up the stairs he stopped halfway, taking note of each of the cars in the lot. The windows to the other rooms were dark or showed the glow of a television set.

He and Freddy made their way up the remaining stairs, unlocked the door to the suite and stepped inside. He had already decided that he would set his alarm to wake every few hours and to sleep on the couch in the living room area of the suite. That way, he would be ready for another attempt on Aubrey's life. He prayed, though, that that would not happen.

SIX

When Aubrey woke up the next morning, she could hear Isaac on the phone in the living room. She washed her face and got dressed, then went into the living room area. Isaac sat in a chair with his laptop open and his phone sitting on the table. Freddy rested at his feet. He greeted Aubrey with several tail thumps on the floor.

He must be trained not to move until Isaac gave him the command.

"I made some coffee, if you want some," he said.

She moved to the counter where the coffeepot was. "Have you been up long?"

"About an hour. Freddy and I went for a quick run, and then I had a conversation with my boss about this case. He's going to put together a video call with the available officers. I'll brief them on the case so far and then see who we can get over here to assist."

"Am I going to be able to go back to work?"

"We'll see," said Isaac. "Certainly not until we can get some protection in place."

Her back stiffened. She was antsy to get back into the field and to assist the other scientists in the lab. "And what will that involve?"

"That's something we'll work through with the other

officers and available resources. We have K-9s whose training is for protection if they are available."

"A dog and an officer would shadow me while I worked? I want to get back up to the site where I was gathering samples." She poured herself a cup of coffee, then took a seat opposite Isaac.

"That is still a crime scene. It would be a challenge to get a whole crime scene crew up there, but we might want to get another set of eyes on it, gather more information and evidence."

Aubrey took a sip of her coffee. More than anything, she wanted to get back to work. But it sounded like everything was up in the air for the moment. "I guess I'll text Mary and let her know I'm not sure if I will be in to work today or not."

He must have sensed her disappointment. His response held a tone of compassion. "We'll try to get you back to work as quickly as possible, but I want you to be safe."

She wrapped her hands around the warm coffee cup. "I get that. It's just that disruption is hard to deal with." She was still concerned about Emily. If she could get to work and Emily was there, maybe her sister really had just been too sick to answer the phone. She had tried calling her again last night before she went to bed and had gotten only voice mail.

"The conference call is in about forty-five minutes. You're welcome to sit in on it and answer any questions the officers might have about what happened to you."

His phone rang. He looked at the number. "It's Jasmin. I'll put her on speakerphone."

Jasmin's voice came across the line. "Hey, I'm going to sit in on the conference call, but I thought you would like to know ahead of time that I have identified two of the men from those files." Jasmin's voice dropped half an octave. "I'm afraid it's not good news."

"Go ahead." Isaac looked up from his phone at Aubrey, who could hear the clicking of computer keys.

"The guy in the coffee shop who lived at that apartment building is Nathan Wharton. His job is repairing arcade games, but he has a record and did some time for hacking and other cybercrimes. The other man, the one who lives in a cabin, is Hans Hilstead, a back-country guide and climbing instructor."

"What is the bad news?"

Jasmin did not answer right away. "Both men are dead."

Aubrey's breath caught in her throat, and she almost dropped her coffee cup. Was Emily in some kind of danger?

Isaac's face had grown pale. "How did they die?"

"Once I had names connected to addresses, I key-worded in the names. Their obituaries came up. They both died two days ago. The obits are vague about cause of death. Both men are under the age of forty, so we can assume it wasn't natural causes. I am going to do some more digging.

"I'm still working on the identity of the other two men," said Jasmin. "I'll let you know as soon as I find out anything. Isaac, is everything okay?"

Isaac's attention was on Aubrey. He reached a hand across the table.

"Just a little bit of a shock to hear that. Hopefully the other two guys can be brought in for questioning, so we can figure out what's going on."

"Has Aubrey been able to get in touch with her sister?"

Aubrey shook her head as tears flooded her eyes.

"Not yet," said Isaac. "See you at the conference call in a bit."

"Sure. I'll let you know then if I've had any new developments," said Jasmin.

Aubrey burst from her seat and retreated to her room to grab her phone. She sent Emily the text that had previously gotten a reply.

R u ok?

She stared at her phone as though that would make her sister respond.

Isaac stood in the doorway. His expression communicated concern. "I know that was hard to hear about those two men. Bear in mind, we don't know anything for sure yet."

"Two men in those photographs are dead. What if those photos are a hit list and Emily is on it? She's still not answering my calls. That text from her might not even be real. The killer could have sent it, so it looked like she was alive." Her hand rested on her pounding heart.

Isaac stepped toward her. "You have to keep your mind on what we know for sure and what we can do to find out more. After this conference call, we can drive over to Emily's place."

Aubrey checked the time. "If she does show up to work, she should be there before the conference call is over. I can call the receptionist and see if she's there. Maybe Emily really was just under the weather. That's my hope anyway."

"Why don't you hang out with Freddy? I'll go rustle us up some breakfast."

Aubrey returned to the living room part of the suite and sat down in one of the plush chairs.

Isaac spoke to Freddy on his way out. "Keep Aubrey company." He grabbed his jacket and headed toward the door but turned back to her. "Remember to bolt the door after I leave. I'll knock three times and say your name when I come back."

Once he was gone, she locked the door.

Isaac's precaution was a reminder of how the threat against her had made her a prisoner. She reached her hand out toward Freddy. "Hey, little buddy."

The dog trotted toward her. Then jumped up so his paws rested on her leg. She stroked his soft head and velvet ears. He sat at her feet. The chair she was in faced the back of the hotel, where the forest was. The trees were only feet from her window.

Her breath caught when she saw movement in the evergreens. She rose to her feet and rushed toward the window just as a person slipped deeper into the forest.

It could just be someone out enjoying nature.

Her heart pounded, and she felt the tickling coolness on the back of her neck, a fear response. She watched, waiting to see if anyone emerged and walked back toward the hotel.

Freddy came to stand beside her and let out a single sharp bark.

She looked down at her floppy-eared friend with the expressive teddy bear eyes. "I know it's kind of scary, isn't it? Glad you're here with me."

She continued to study the area outside, still not seeing anyone. The man who came after her had managed to find out they were in the lower level room. He might find out they had moved upstairs through whatever means he had used the first time. What if he had been watching her window?

She jumped when she heard the three knocks at the

door. Isaac said her name, and she moved across the floor and twisted the dead bolt.

Just knowing he was close helped her to calm down. "Everything all right?"

He must have seen something in her face.

She turned slightly. "I just thought I saw someone in the trees." She tilted her head to indicate the window. "But I'm not sure."

Isaac set the food down and hurried to look where she had indicated. After a long moment, he drew the curtains shut. "This is why I need to get you more protection. If I have any indication he knows we moved to a more secure room, we're out of here."

Her heart flooded with gratitude over how protective he was of her. "It might have just been someone hiking through the trees. I'm on edge."

"Understandable." He walked back toward where he put down the bag that contained the food. "I got us each a full breakfast. Scrambled eggs, sausage, orange juice for me, and I remember you liked tomato juice."

She laughed. "'Cause I'm a weirdo." It was a joke from ten years ago when they would go out to breakfast and talk about her preference for an unconventional breakfast drink. When he used to tease her about it, her response was always to say *'Cause I'm a weirdo.*

He smiled at first and then his expression grew serious while he took the food containers out and placed them on the table.

What was he thinking about? Maybe he was just focused on the current investigation, or it could be that any mention of the past caused him to withdraw.

She stepped toward him and touched his back. "I'm just glad you remembered what I like for breakfast."

He nodded and sat down. It felt as though the temperature in the room had dropped. What was this strange dance they were doing? Feeling so connected one minute and then one or both of them putting up walls the next.

The past is gone. Stay in the now, Aubrey.

When she opened her to-go container, the spicy fragrance of the sausage reached her nose. There was also toast.

Isaac pushed the jam and butter packets toward her.

"This looks wonderful," she said.

"Thought we should have something hearty since we don't know when we'll eat again. The day might end up being busy."

Aubrey took her plastic knife and buttered the toast. She opened her can of tomato juice and took a sip.

Freddy sat between the two of them, watching each bite they took and then letting out a little whine when either of them looked his way.

"He's been taught to only take food from my hand, and people food is not good for him." Isaac leaned over and petted Freddy. "I think the smell is just making him a little hungry."

They finished their breakfast, cleaned up and got ready for the conference call.

Isaac opened his laptop and pulled an empty chair close to his. She sat down beside him close enough that their shoulders brushed against each other. His proximity brought back the memories of embraces, kisses, promises and plans.

Was it possible that they had fallen for each other so hard and so quickly, the intensity of it could not have been sustained? Even without his mother's interference, they probably would have broken up. It just would have taken longer.

At eighteen, she had seen Isaac as a sort of rescuer,

someone who could give her what she had always longed for, identity and a family. In the ten years since, she had forged her own life, and she knew who she was. She was no longer that needy young woman desperate to feel loved.

As the faces of the other members of the K-9 team came on the screen, Aubrey took in a breath and prayed for resolution to the attacks that had taken away her freedom.

Isaac adjusted the brightness of his screen as Asher Gilmore, Ruby Orton and Jasmin Eastwood all appeared on the screen in separate boxes. The chief had not been able to attend due to a conflict.

Both Asher and Ruby were in uniform. Asher ran his fingers through his light brown hair and smiled. Ruby's long brown hair just touched her shoulders. Isaac was used to seeing it in a low bun. She wore a gold necklace that offset her nutmeg-colored skin. Jasmin was wearing her usual red lipstick, all the more striking with her brown eyes and dark skin. The crisp high-collared shirt just touched her pixie-cut hair.

"Thank you all for being available. I know the chief said he would give you a brief summary of why I am asking for more support up here at Mount St. Helens. Jasmin and I will fill you in on what we know so far and answer any questions you might have." He turned slightly toward Aubrey. "This is Aubrey Smith. She's the woman who was attacked three times."

Isaac detailed the attacks and finding the thumb drive and then turned it over to Jasmin, who summarized what they knew so far about the photos on the drive.

"We still don't have any idea what connects these five people other than that Emily is currently employed by the foundation and the first two attacks and the dropped thumb drive were all in that area." Isaac was sitting close enough to Aubrey that he felt her stiffen when Emily's name was mentioned.

"There is something else, but we don't know if it is connected," Aubrey said. "One of the scientists I work with believes that someone may have been on the research side of the foundation a few nights before someone came after me."

"But there was no sign of forced entry," added Isaac. "No sign that anything had been taken."

"So that could just be a big nothing burger." Ruby's Southern accent snuck into her words despite the fact she had lived in the Northwest for years.

"I just thought it was worth mentioning," said Aubrey.

"My immediate concern right now is some extra protection for Aubrey so I can work this case. The area where the first attack happened is not easily accessible. Getting a whole crime scene team up there might not be feasible, but I would like to take another K-9 team member up there and have a deeper look around."

"I can come this afternoon," said Ruby.

"I'm knee-deep in some underwater narcotics detection training with Spark," said Asher. "But I think Tanner is close to wrapping up an investigation. He might be available to get up there in the next day or so."

"It would be good if we could get two K-9 teams up here today," said Isaac, "to provide additional protection and look at the crime scene."

Jasmin spoke up. "I think Brandie and her dog Taz could use some more field experience."

"Brandie Weller is one of four candidates who are hoping to be hired for the two slots that we have open on the PNK9 team," Isaac explained to Aubrey.

"I'll get in touch with Donovan to see if he thinks Brandie would be a good choice," said Ruby.

"Great then," said Isaac. "Are there any developments in the double homicide?"

Isaac, like the rest of the team, was hoping there would be some word from Mara, their rookie CSI who was the prime suspect and still in hiding. Isaac found it impossible to believe that Mara had killed her ex-boyfriend and his new girlfriend, no matter how bad the evidence against her was. His gut told him so.

The team was missing something when it came to why Mara wasn't coming forward—and she'd hinted at it a few weeks ago in a text to her half brother, fellow PNK9 officer Asher Gilmore, from a burner phone while professing her innocence. Something to do with their father, who was in a nursing home. Asher had said he'd follow up on that and hopefully had information for the team today.

Isaac would never forget the chills he'd gotten when Asher had shared the text Mara had sent: *I didn't kill Jonas and Stacey. I can't say more. Dad's life depends on it. And so does yours. I'm sorry.*

The team *had* to solve the murders so that Mara could finally come home. But it was clear she wouldn't until her life and Asher's father's were no longer in danger.

Asher was the first to speak up. "After Mara sent that text to me saying she was innocent and she was worried our father was in danger, I did go to the nursing home where he is staying and talked to the staff."

Isaac knew that there was contention between the siblings because Asher hadn't visited his father since he'd been admitted to the home due to dementia. Mara and Asher hadn't grown up together and weren't close, though Isaac knew they'd both been working on that earlier this year. Mara had only been with the unit for six months before she'd fled, so the siblings' relationship was fledgling at best. "Did you get a chance to say hello to your dad?"

"Why? He won't know who I am." Asher's tone was defensive.

For sure, there was pain connected to trying to have a relationship with a parent whose memory was unstable, but it still seemed like Asher should have made the effort since he was in the facility.

Jasmin, ever the peacemaker, spoke in a soft voice. "Did you find out anything?"

"I wanted to check on my dad's safety, see if anyone had tried to hurt him. Anyway, it turns out one of the employees said my father did have a visitor who came in and asked for him by name." Asher shook his head. "The staff member said that the guy didn't talk to my dad, just stood off at a distance and took a picture of him while he sat out on the lawn in his wheelchair in that yellow sweater he wears all the time."

"Did the employee at the home remember what the guy looked like?" Ruby asked.

"Yeah, the female LPN I spoke to described him as being in his early thirties with brown hair, a friendly disposition and expensively dressed, that he looked like he worked out. I could tell from the way she described him she was a little smitten," said Asher. "The clincher, though, was she mentioned his cornflower blue eyes. Who does that sound like to you?"

"Eli Ballard," said Jasmin.

Isaac watched Ruby's expression change at the mention of Eli's name. Her new boyfriend—and the Mount Rainier National Park female murder victim's former business partner. Eli now owned the three Stark Lodges with Stacey's brother.

It was clear that Asher hadn't known Ruby was dating

Eli or he would have spoken to her privately about what he'd learned before sharing it with the team.

Could Eli be involved in the murders of Stacey Stark and her boyfriend, Jonas Digby? Was he himself the killer? What was his connection to Mara and Asher's father? Why would he visit the man in his nursing home?

Isaac thought back to how the murders of Stacey Stark and Jonas Digby had been reported in the first place. A witness called 911, claiming to see a woman with dark hair and a blue down jacket shoot the young couple by a bridge in the park. But the witness had refused to give his name and the call had been untraceable. Had it been Eli Ballard, the real killer who'd framed Mara? Had he lured her out there as the perfect person to pin the murders on?

So many questions and no answers.

Isaac didn't know what to think. Eli had been ruled out as a suspect early on in the investigation, but it was easy enough to set up an alibi and *seem* helpful in answering questions.

For Ruby's sake, he hoped Eli wasn't the killer. But why else would a man matching Eli Ballard's description be at the nursing home when Mara had said that her father's life—and brother's—depended on her staying in hiding? Had Eli threatened to hurt her dad and Asher if she came forward?

"I don't know, there might be something there," said Jasmin. "Eli was not only Stacey's business partner, but do you remember last month when Willow Bates said her K-9 alerted on the locked basement door at the lodge in Olympic Park? Star is trained to detect firearms. Willow said that Eli told her that the family hunting rifles were in the basement, but he wouldn't let her go down there to look. And when he finally did, something just seemed off."

"Eli might be up to something," Isaac said, finding it difficult to look at Ruby. She had to be very upset but was too professional to show it. "It's hard to understand his motive since the lodges weren't in good financial shape and his new partner, Stacey's brother, isn't even sure he wants a stake in the business. Eli and Stacey were good friends, as far as everyone associated with either of them knew. Why would he kill her—and her boyfriend? And what's his connection to Mara and Asher's father?" Isaac watched as Ruby acted distracted staring down, either taking notes or looking at her phone. "We have to follow every lead."

"For sure," said Asher. "Anyway, I'm going to have our father moved to a safe house. Maybe that will make Mara feel like she can come out of hiding if I can find a way to contact her."

Jasmin piped up. "We're still trying to trace the phone that Mara texted Asher from. I don't think it's real hopeful, since it was a burner phone. With her father's and brother's lives threatened, I can understand why she's staying in the shadows."

"I can take care of myself," Asher said. "But our father can't. I'll get him moved today to a safe location with a good team of nursing care."

There was a long silence. Aubrey got up and moved to pour herself another cup of coffee.

Isaac stared at the screen. "Is there anything else I need to be kept in the loop about?"

Asher and Jasmin shook their heads.

Though she still seemed distracted, Ruby lifted her head. "I have an update on the missing bloodhound puppies that Peyton and I got a tip on." Peyton was the team's lead trainer for the dogs. Back in June, the three puppies that were gifted to the unit and in the process of being trained as K-9s had been stolen from the training center. The pups had been only months away from being placed with handlers.

"I take it none of the leads panned out or you would have told us right away," said Isaac.

"I'd been hoping the lead about the backyard breeder as the thief would turn out to be true, but when I went to check that out, the puppies weren't there. Pepper didn't alert on anything to indicate they had ever been there. So, dead end."

"Something will come up," said Asher. "They couldn't have vanished into thin air."

"Ruby, I'll see you this afternoon and maybe Brandie as well," Isaac said.

"Sure," said Ruby. Her response had a hollow ring to it as if her mind were elsewhere, and Isaac knew it was. She glanced up and then wiggled in her seat.

The conference call was not a place to bring up personal issues even when they intersected with investigations. Ruby clearly was very upset that Eli was likely their new prime suspect in the double homicide. Isaac hoped he could talk with her privately once she got here.

He signed off from the meeting as each of the others disappeared from the screen as well.

His mind was still on Ruby. He thought of her as a sister and was worried the news about Eli would wreck her. He sent her a text.

Chin up. You have done nothing wrong as far as Eli is concerned. We had no way of knowing.

Ruby texted back right away.

Thanks for your support. Still, I wish I had a better track record where men are concerned. Boy can I pick them.

Don't blame yourself, Ruby. Eli fooled us all. See you in a bit. Take care.

He was sure he'd get a chance to talk to Ruby some more, not just about her situation but his own. Some of the other team members were aware that a woman he'd been serious about had broken up with him by text ten years ago. He could use Ruby's input about Aubrey and having her back in his life—even just as a case.

When he looked up, Aubrey was holding her phone and pacing.

"I just called Mary, the receptionist at work. My sister should have been at work twenty minutes ago. I sent Emily another text. She hasn't responded."

"Let's go by her place and see if she's still home sick," said Isaac.

Aubrey nodded. "I hope that's all that is going on. I flip-flop from being suspicious of my sister to worried that she's in terrible danger."

"Only one way to get an answer to that question," said Isaac. "We need to find your sister."

SEVEN

Aubrey tried to clear her mind and calm down, as she recited Emily's address so Isaac could punch it into his GPS. She'd grabbed the key for Emily's apartment, which her sister had trusted her with.

She stared through the windshield and watched the road zip by as the morning sun warmed her face. More than anything, she wanted to have a relationship with her sister. Accusing her of something she may or may not be involved in or casting suspicions would not help mend things between them.

They arrived at the apartment building where Emily lived. Only a few cars were parked on the street, and none of them were Emily's.

Aubrey pointed toward the building. "Her place is a ground level apartment, number 5." The doors opened directly onto the street, like a motel.

They headed up the sidewalk with Freddy heeling at Isaac's side. Aubrey knocked on the door. After a few minutes, she knocked again and then put the key in the lock.

"Let me go in first," said Isaac.

His hand touched where his gun was concealed briefly before he opened the door and stepped inside.

Aubrey followed. "Em, it's me, Aubrey."

She braced herself as she took another step where she had view of the living room. She half expected to see signs of a break-in or a struggle.

The place was dark, and the curtains were drawn. Nothing looked out of place. Isaac stepped in behind her.

"I'll go check the bedroom." Tension threaded through her chest as she headed down the hallway. The bedroom door was open only a crack. She knocked. "Emily?"

She pushed the door open. The bed was made and there was no sign of Emily. When she checked her sister's closet, the one suitcase Emily owned was still there, and it didn't look like any clothes had been taken. Her toiletry items were neatly organized in the bathroom.

She returned to the living room/kitchen area. Isaac was in the kitchen looking at the garbage under the sink. "There are no signs that your sister was here this morning. No fresh garbage, or a breakfast plate in the sink." He walked over to the counter and pulled the basket where the grounds were in the coffee maker. "Doesn't look like anyone made coffee this morning. No mug in the sink. No dishes in the dishwasher. From the looks of the place your sister is pretty tidy, but I would say she didn't come back here yesterday."

"Emily is kind of a neat freak." A memory flashed through Aubrey's head of her sister vacuuming and dusting in the tiny room they had shared at the first foster home they'd been placed in. "I think having everything in place creates a sense of calm for her." Emily's toiletries were still in the bathroom and she hadn't even come back for clothes. Was she afraid to come back? "Her story about being under the weather probably is not true."

"She likes plants, I see." Isaac pointed to the abundance of greenery in the living room.

"Yes, that's why I have a key. If she had to go away

for a few days, she wanted me to water her plants. I think giving me the key was mostly to show trust. It's strange that the curtains are drawn. Emily always worried about the plants getting enough light. Honestly, that is the only thing that seems out of character for Emily to do." Aubrey stared at the curtains. "Maybe she didn't want someone looking in."

Freddy snorted. Nose to the floor he paced into the living room, up the hallway and then back into the kitchen.

"Something has him riled," said Aubrey.

"I haven't given the command for him to do anything." Isaac squatted on the floor and called Freddy over. "He's smelling something. Maybe a scent that he's been exposed to previously."

Freddy nuzzled his nose against Isaac's jacket pocket and then sat down.

"What's in your pocket?"

"The thumb drive. I still haven't had a chance to get it to my team to be analyzed."

Aubrey shook her head. "What is he trying to tell us?"

"Dogs' noses can separate out smells. He's trained to detect the chemical on the electronics, but he could also smell the scent of whoever touched the thumb drive."

"So you're saying whoever held that thumb drive was in my sister's place."

"It's just a guess. Based on what Freddy is trying to communicate."

Aubrey slumped down in a chair. "If she is in some kind of danger, why won't she just communicate with me? Doesn't she know I would help her?" Maybe Emily didn't believe that. From an early age, they both had learned to be self-sufficient in order to survive. Emily had a lot of shame about her past. Maybe she feared Aubrey would bring it up if she came for help.

"I hate to ask this question, but what kind of stuff was Emily involved in before she reconciled with you?"

"Petty theft and drugs. Emily's big weakness is choosing the wrong guy to be involved with."

"Was she seeing anyone?"

"I don't think so, but I'm not sure. My sister could be secretive. I want things to be better between us. We have a lot to work through, but I didn't want to be pushy or nosy and cause her to back off from the relationship." She put her face in her hands and shook her head. "I don't want to let my mind go there, but what if she has done something terrible and has just run off?"

Isaac crossed the room, sat down beside Aubrey and rubbed her back. "We don't know anything for sure yet."

"I want to think the best of her. She seemed genuine when she got in touch with me and said she wanted to turn her life around." His touch kept her from bursting into tears. Years ago, his being close had always made her feel calm and confident. Some things didn't change.

Freddy let out a sympathetic whine, put his front paws on the sofa and licked her hand. It was nice to have so much support.

Isaac wrapped his arm around her back and squeezed her shoulder. "It's going to be okay. We'll find her."

She rested her face against his shoulder. "I'm really afraid."

"I get that. If it was my brother who seemed to have disappeared, I'd feel the same way," said Isaac.

Being held by Isaac, hearing the warmth of his voice, made her realize that she had missed having him in her life. He always had a way of talking her off her emotional ledges. She pulled away, not wanting the moment of connection to cross any lines.

He rose to his feet, indicating that he, too, must have

wanted to keep things just friendly and supportive. He cleared his throat. "Ruby should be getting to the foundation by the time we drive over there. If Brandle was able to come, you can maybe work inside while Ruby and I head back up to where you were shot at."

She longed to get back out in the field, but she would take what she could get. There was plenty she could work on inside the facility as well.

Isaac headed toward the door and opened it. He stared outside and then shut the door. His features hardened.

"Is something wrong?"

"When we came here, there was a man sitting on the bench in that park across the street with a view of Emily's front door. One of the cars has been moved, and that same man is now sitting behind the wheel."

Fear shot through her like an arrow. "Do you suppose he was watching this place?"

"Now his car is positioned for a quick pullout, probably to follow the K-9 vehicle," said Isaac.

"He must be watching Emily's place. Why? Who is he?"

Isaac pulled his gun from the holster. "I don't know but I'm going to find out. You stay in here with Freddy. Lock the door behind me."

Once he stepped outside, Isaac slipped behind a hedge before the man in the car had a chance to turn his head and see him. The driver's attention was on the K-9 vehicle. He was clearly waiting for Isaac and Aubrey to come out. If he was watching for Emily, maybe he thought they would lead him to her. Or that Aubrey was Emily because from a distance they looked alike.

Even though it was clear from the driver's actions what he was up to, Isaac did not have probable cause for arresting or even questioning him. It wasn't illegal to sit in your car on a city street. Plus he might be armed.

If the man in the car did tail them, Isaac could stop him for suspicious activity and harassment of a police officer.

Crouching and walking in a straight line from the hedge so he was shielded from view, Isaac retreated back to the apartment. He knocked lightly. Aubrey opened the door almost immediately.

"You and Freddy come with me," he said. "Stay on my far side so you're shielded from the man in the car." If his intent was to shoot at them, he didn't want Aubrey to be an easy target. "Just act natural. We're going to see if this guy will follow us. Right now, he hasn't done anything that he couldn't lie his way out of if I questioned him."

When Isaac did a quick glance in the direction of the car, the driver had slipped down below the dashboard. He didn't realize that Isaac had already made him.

They got in the SUV. Isaac started the car and drove. At first, he didn't see anyone in the rearview mirror. Once he got through the residential neighborhood, though, he saw the car behind them. Isaac pulled into the parking lot of a convenience store. The other car rolled by on the street.

Aubrey turned in her seat. "He lost us."

"He'll be back. That's a trick in tailing someone. He'll assume that we've gone into the store, circle back and wait for us to pull out. Get down low so he doesn't see our heads." Isaac watched his side and rearview mirror. In less than a minute, the car tailing them parked on the street by the convenience store. "Stay in here. Lock the doors."

Isaac slipped around to the front of the car and then circled around the convenience store so the man tailing them wouldn't see him coming. With his hand hovering over his gun, Isaac approached the driver.

The man rolled down the window. "Officer?"

Isaac had half expected the guy to either shoot at him or drive away.

"Are you in the habit of following a police officer in a harassing manner? You want to tell me why you're tailing me?"

"I'm a PI. I was hired to stake out Emily Smith's house and report when she showed up. You guys were the first action I had gotten in twenty-four hours. I thought you might lead me to her."

The guy seemed to be sincere.

"If you let me reach for my wallet, I'll show you my license," said the man.

Isaac nodded. "Who hired you?"

"I don't know. The request was made via my website. Once the fee is paid, I go to work, and I don't ask any questions." He showed Isaac his credentials and handed him a business card.

Isaac took note of the man's name. "Were you given a phone number to contact once Emily Smith showed up?"

"Yes," said the PI.

"I'll need that number." Isaac pulled out his phone and typed in the number in the notes section. It was probably a number from a burner phone, but he'd have Jasmin trace it all the same. Someone who wanted to remain anonymous through a website probably wouldn't give a phone number that could be connected back to him or her.

The PI seemed to want to cooperate. Isaac suspected he was telling the truth.

"Emily Smith is a person of interest in an ongoing investigation." Isaac pulled out one of his cards. "I suggest if you do locate her, you contact us first."

The PI agreed and Isaac stepped away from his car. As he walked across the lot, Aubrey pushed the button to unlock the doors of Isaac's SUV.

"Well?"

"He's a private investigator hired to watch Emily's place and notify the client when she shows up."

"That's bad news and good news," said Aubrey. "It means someone is trying to track down Emily. But they haven't found her yet."

Isaac's phone pinged that he had a text. It was from Brandie, one of the candidates for the PNK9 open slot, who'd be helping Ruby on his case.

About five minutes away from the foundation research building.

An earlier text from Ruby that he must have missed informed him that she had been delayed.

"Your protection is waiting for you if you want to go back to work in the building."

"That would be great. I have things I can work on at my desk and in the lab," said Aubrey.

Isaac started his K-9 vehicle and pulled out toward the road that led back to Mount St. Helens. "You'll like Brandie. She doesn't talk a lot about herself, but the little bit I've seen of her working with Taz, that's the German shepherd she's been assigned to train with, makes me think she'd be good K-9 handler."

"You mean she's not a full-fledged K-9 officer yet?" A little fear had crept into Aubrey's voice.

"She is. I just meant I haven't worked closely with her. All four candidates have to put in some hours with the rest of the team. Not only do they have to be good K-9 officers, but they have to mesh with the other officers." He found himself wishing that he could be the one to watch over Aubrey at the foundation so she wasn't afraid, but if he could move the investigation forward, she wouldn't need protection at all.

After Isaac pulled into the employee parking lot of the foundation, they both got out of the vehicle. Isaac glanced around, not seeing another K-9 SUV. He pulled his phone out and started to text. "I wonder if Brandie parked on the public side of the foundation. I forgot to tell her to park in employee parking."

Aubrey moved toward the door while Isaac finished his text. She turned back to face him as if she had thought of something. Her expression changed when something over his shoulder caught her attention.

"That's Emily's car. She's here." Aubrey flung the door open and rushed inside.

Isaac hurried after her. Maybe now they would get some answers.

EIGHT

Aubrey flew through the door. Emily's desk was behind a partition not visible from the entrance. She ran across the room. Emily's phone sat beside her computer and a sweater was hung on the back of the chair, but her sister wasn't there.

Isaac had followed her in. She stepped from behind the partition and shook her head. Emily was around here somewhere.

Mary came up a hallway, holding a stack of folders. "Aubrey, your text implied that you probably weren't coming in today."

"Everything is a little up in the air right now. Is my sister here?"

"I meant to call you, but we've been so busy. She showed up maybe an hour ago."

"Where is she now?"

Mary set the folders on the counter. "I asked her earlier to go over to the gift shop to collect their invoices. That might be where she is."

The foundation had two sides, a private higher security side where Aubrey worked and the public side where there were exhibits, a gift shop and opportunity to sign up for tours or listen to a ranger or volcanologist talk.

Aubrey hurried toward the door that led to the public

side of the foundation. She opened it, stepped through and ran up the hallway; the place was already teeming with people. Assuming that Isaac was behind her, she pushed through the crowd and hurried toward the busy gift shop.

She stood on tiptoe, trying to see above the people and get the clerk's attention. The clerk was focused on ringing up a customer's purchase.

Aubrey turned around. She didn't see Isaac anywhere. Several people bumped into her as she tried to make her way out of the gift shop.

When the crowd dispersed, Aubrey saw Emily across the room with her back turned. As if she knew someone was staring, Emily pivoted, her gaze landing on Aubrey. Her sister's expression darkened. Aubrey recognized that look of shame. Emily darted toward the entrance, leaving the pile of papers she'd been holding on a display case.

Aubrey pushed through the crowd. Once outside, the sun nearly blinded her. She drew a protective hand up to her face. The parking lot and surrounding area was just as busy as inside. She scanned in all directions, looking for her sister. A flash of purple by a tour bus caught her eye. Emily had been wearing a purple dress.

She ran in that direction.

A hand grabbed her arm from behind. She swung around to see Isaac. "It's not safe for you to be out in the open like this. You need to go back inside."

"It's Emily. I saw her. She's here."

"You go back inside. Brandie and Taz are over there. We'll do the searching."

"But my sister—"

"You can't be out in this crowd. Go back to the work side of the foundation and wait. I'll text you if we find her. Where did you see her last?"

A young dark-haired woman holding the leash of a German shepherd was crossing the parking lot.

"That way." Aubrey pointed. "She's wearing a purple dress."

Isaac nodded, then he and Freddy ran toward Brandie and Taz.

Someone pushed Aubrey from the back.

"Oh, sorry," said a man's voice.

When she turned to see who it was, the man had already been engulfed by a crowd of people.

The little accident had caused her heart to race. Isaac was right. As much as she wanted to find her sister, she'd be safer inside. Knowing she couldn't get back through to where she worked because the door only opened into the visitor side, she walked around the building back to the work side of the foundation.

Her stomach churned from anxiety. She returned to the desk where Emily had been working. She picked up her sister's phone, tempted to check the calling and texting history if it wasn't password protected. But she caught herself. Violating her sister's privacy would not build trust. Emily was here. She had come into work, but something had frightened her when she saw Aubrey.

Aubrey looked closer at the wallpaper that was on the phone, half-concealed by apps and icons.

A chill ran over her skin. The photo was of Emily and a man, in profile, sitting at an outdoor café. She looked closer. Her breath caught. The picture had been taken at night, but she was pretty sure she was looking at a man who was on the thumb drive, Nathan Wharton. The one with a record for hacking and cybercrimes. The dead man. Her heart squeezed tight. What had her sister gotten involved with?

She held the phone to her chest, closed her eyes and prayed.

Please keep Emily safe.

And yet Emily had come back to work today. As if she was trying to do the right thing. She had fled when she knew Aubrey was here.

Mary's voice came from behind her. "Everything okay?"

"Did my sister say anything to you when she came in?"

"You know, I think she came in to talk to Duncan. It was after I told her you weren't coming into work that she said something about needing the hours."

"Why did she want to talk to Duncan?"

"Not sure. She asked where he was the first thing when she came in. I saw the two of them through the glass wall of his office. The conversation looked intense, but I wouldn't say it looked like a fight. I have no idea what they were talking about," Mary said. "The other times I saw them interacting they always seemed friendly."

"Thanks." When Aubrey crossed the room to Duncan's office, she found it locked. She walked to her boss's office, where Leandra Ware was sitting in front of her computer. "Duncan was here this morning. Do you know where he went?"

"He didn't say anything to me. You can check the sign-out sheet. Maybe he was doing some on-site research. I don't believe he was scheduled to give any talks to the tourists today."

Grabbing her mug, Leandra pushed her chair back, stood up and walked over to her coffee maker. She filled her cup and returned to her desk. "You look a bit out of sorts. Did anything get resolved with those attacks on you?"

"Not yet." Aubrey gave only a brief summary of what she and Isaac had uncovered. "I don't suppose the park police have gotten back to you on the break-in."

Leandra shook her head and then took a sip of her coffee. "Potential break-in. You know how Christopher can be about everything being in place. It might all be in his imagination."

"What about the handprint on the glass downstairs? Was it matched with someone who works at the foundation?"

"I haven't heard anything on that yet," said Leandra. "They haven't asked for any one of us to give a fingerprint sample. They must still be working on it."

Aubrey excused herself and wandered across the floor to check the sign-out sheet. Duncan had gone up to a part of the volcano where the cell service would be nonexistent. He was not Aubrey's favorite person, as he could be condescending and quick to remind her that he was the head researcher and the one with the PhD. That didn't mean Duncan was guilty of anything or that Emily's behavior had anything to do with the conversation Mary had observed.

She walked over to where the receptionist sat in front of a desktop computer. "If Emily or Duncan come back, please let me know right away."

"Where will you be?"

"Inside somewhere?" Aubrey wandered into her own office and sat down, trying to clear her mind. She'd come here to work, and now she wasn't sure if she would even be able to focus.

Through the glass of her office, she watched as Brandie, Isaac and their K-9 partners entered the building. She could not read their expressions, but Emily was not with them. She rose from her chair and rushed over to find out what was going on.

Isaac introduced Aubrey to Brandie and Taz. "We didn't find Emily. But her car is still in the lot. She couldn't have gotten far on foot. Do you have something that has Emily's scent on it?"

Aubrey moved to the carrel where Emily's desk was, pulled a sweater off the back of the chair and handed it to Isaac.

He glanced in Brandie's direction. "And we need a picture of her so Brandie knows what she looks like."

"I have one in my office." Aubrey pivoted and then turned back. "Actually, I think you should see this." Aubrey picked up the phone sitting on Emily's desk. "You can't see Emily clearly, but it's who is with her that is concerning."

Brandie and Isaac moved in closer to look at the phone screen.

Isaac cleared his throat. "Is that who I think it is?"

Aubrey nodded as her forehead creased with worry.

Emily had known the dead man Nathan Wharton, well enough to have dinner with him. Nathan had a criminal record. The picture was the type people took on dates. He tried to alleviate the rising tension settling in his chest by taking a deep breath. This did not look good for Emily. By falling for a guy with a criminal record, she was either in danger or involved with something nefarious.

Brandie drew the phone closer to her face. "I don't understand."

She had probably not been briefed on the details of the case. Only told that she had an opportunity for field training.

"I'll explain later," said Isaac. "The clock is ticking for finding Emily. Let's go."

Brandie headed toward the door with the sweater.

"Let me get the picture from my office. You can take it with you." Aubrey was gone only a few minutes. She returned with the photo, which was no longer in its frame.

Isaac turned back toward Aubrey. The look of devastation on her face made him want to take her in his arms.

He gave Aubrey a hug. He couldn't tell her that everything was going to be okay. That might be a lie. "We will do our best to find your sister."

She melted against him for a moment, and he was reminded of how good it felt to hold her in his arms. "I know you will." She pulled away and looked into his eyes.

He brushed his hand over her cheek and turned to where Brandie was waiting for him at the door. When they stepped outside, Ruby had just pulled up in her K-9 vehicle. Her black Lab, Pepper, specialized in search and rescue and would be able to track even better than the other two dogs. When Ruby got out and deployed her dog, she also took out a sticky roller to get the dog hair off her pant legs. Isaac knew from working with Ruby that dog hair bugged her, and she had a bottomless supply of rollers.

Isaac ran over to her and explained the situation. He handed over Emily's sweater and showed her the picture. "I'll stay close with Brandie and see how she does. You and Pepper can start on the east side of the building. We'll take the west."

"Gotcha." Ruby placed the sweater beneath Pepper's nose. The dog wagged her tail once, let out an abbreviated whine, put her nose to the ground and took off.

Isaac and Brandie headed toward the other side of the building, which connected with the trail that people hiked as well as viewing areas. Ruby would be working her way toward the road that eventually led out of the park.

The dogs kept their noses to the ground but never pulled hard on the leashes, which meant they hadn't matched the smell on the sweater to any scent as their keen noses sorted through hundreds of smells. They worked their way all around the busy parking lot.

Isaac stopped and Freddy sat down beside him. He radioed Ruby. "Anything?"

Ruby's voice came through the radio. "Negative."

Emily couldn't have just vanished into thin air. The scent trail of where she'd gone was here. But with all the people milling around it might be hard for the dogs to pick it up.

Brandie glanced over her shoulder and stopped as well, drawing closer to Isaac so they could talk. "I'm going back into the public side of the foundation where we know Emily last was to see if Freddy can pick up the trail that way. Why don't you see if you can find anything on the outskirts of the parking lot?"

Brandie nodded. "Can do. Come on, Taz." She took off with her K-9.

Isaac entered the building where the exhibits and gift shop were. Freddy pulled on the leash, leading him to the gift shop and then back out the door. The scent was still here. Once outside, Freddy slowed down but continued to circle back to the entrance and then out again, going a little farther every time.

He caught a glimpse of Brandie as she headed up toward the first viewing area. She and Taz trotted at a good pace. A tour van blocked his view for a moment as it backed up. The van stopped suddenly, the brakes squealing. Taz came into view running a few feet one way and then in the other direction. His leash dragged on the ground. Where had Brandie gone? The van driver stopped and jumped out, running to where a crowd gathered.

Isaac and Freddy sprinted toward the cluster of people and an agitated Taz. He pushed through the crowd to find Brandie being helped to her feet. She brushed off her dirty knees where gravel had stuck to her pants.

"What happened?"

"I'm not sure." Taz ran toward Brandie, and she grabbed his leash.

The crowd slowly dispersed. Brandie's expression indicated she was shaken up by her fall. Her hands as well had been scuffed up by the gravel.

He glanced around and spotted a bench. "Let's go sit down, so you can catch your breath."

"We have a job to do." Brandie reached out to touch Taz's head.

"You were almost run over. We can take a moment for you to recover."

He led her over to the bench. They both sat down, and the dogs took up positions by the feet of their respective partners.

"Tell me what happened," said Isaac.

When Brandie pushed a strand of brown hair behind her ear, he saw that her hand was shaking. "Taz and I were clipping along at a good pace. I saw that van backing up out of the corner of my eye. We were well clear of it and then—" She took in a ragged breath and looked at Isaac. "I think someone pushed me."

"Are you sure about that?"

"There was a crowd of people. I felt a weight press against my back."

"I suppose it could have been an accident."

Brandie nodded. "It's just that now I am the third of

the four candidates who had their work sabotaged. Owen got that fake text that made him leave his post at the safe house and Veronica was delayed right when she needed to go on assignment. That just leaves Parker who hasn't been made to look bad."

Isaac mentally shook his head. With only two open spots in the esteemed PNK9 unit and four hopefuls, could one of them be behind the sabotage to wipe out some competition? Parker was a braggart, but was he necessarily guilty? "This is escalating though. This is the first time one of the candidates could have been physically harmed...or worse." Isaac could not hide his ire. This had to stop.

Freddy rose to his feet and licked his chops, jerking on the leash slightly. Isaac let Freddy lead him a few feet away from the bench back to the area where the van had nearly backed over Brandie.

A napkin lay on the ground. It had the logo for a B and B. He picked it up and carried it back to where Brandie had risen to her feet. He showed it to her. "That's the B and B where Parker is staying while he does some field training over in Olympic National Park."

"Bit of a drive from here," said Isaac. "Look, I know this sabotage has been an ongoing thing. Maybe we can set up some kind of conference call and clear the air once and for all. See if we can find a time when the chief can sit in."

Brandie nodded. "I want to give Parker the benefit of the doubt, but it's strange that he hasn't been affected by the sabotage."

Isaac didn't say anything, but Brandie could have just as easily staged the accident and dropped the napkin. "If I can do anything to make sure the training isn't disrupted again, and we can weed out the candidate behind this troublemaking, I will help."

"Thank you. I appreciate that." The guarded quality that usually permeated Brandie's conversations was no longer there. Maybe his support of her had built a little trust with the candidate who had come across as competent but a bit cagey. He wondered too if Brandie's standoffishness was because of something she was trying to hide.

Ruby's voice came across the radio. "Hey, guys, I'm headed back toward the building. I think I might have figured something out."

Isaac spoke into the radio. "We'll meet you down there."

As they trotted back toward the public side of the foundation, he wondered what Ruby and Pepper had discovered. He found himself thinking about Aubrey as well. Knowing that Emily had spent time with one of the men whose photo was on that thumb drive had clearly shaken Aubrey up. Though his professional obligations had pulled him away, Isaac had wanted to stay with her longer to make sure she was okay.

Maybe what Ruby had figured out would help them find Emily and get to the bottom of her involvement in this.

NINE

Aubrey headed downstairs to one of the labs to do testing on samples that had been gathered from another site, not the one where she'd been shot at. Separating the trace minerals within these samples would give her something to compare to once she was able to go back to the site, which she thought might yield different results.

She opened the door and stepped inside. This was the older lab that Christopher had said had a smear on the glass that was a handprint. The glass that looked in on the lab clearly had been cleaned since then.

As she gathered the materials she needed, her thoughts kept spinning back to Emily and her confusing behavior. Though Aubrey knew her focus wouldn't be 100 percent, she needed to do something to get her mind off everything that had happened.

The lab consisted of two rooms, the larger one that looked out on the basement hallway and a small windowless room where she would be working.

She ground up the first sample until it was the consistency of coarse sand and then laid it out on a slide that she'd placed a label on.

She heard a noise in the larger room. She moved to see who it was when her door shut suddenly. She walked across the room and tried the knob. It wouldn't budge.

She banged on the door with a flat hand. "Hey, whoever is out there, you shut me in here." Her heart pounded. Her phone was upstairs on her desk. She'd forgotten to grab it. She jiggled the knob again. Fear descended as she listened to someone moving around in the larger room. "What's going on out there?"

This wasn't another scientist or an intern who had absentmindedly closed the door. Someone had locked her in on purpose. She had never noticed but the door must lock from the outside, or some kind of weight or wedge had been put against it. The doorknob had screws on the plate. Maybe she could somehow disengage the lock if she could get the knob off.

A strange smell invaded the room as she opened drawers, searching for a screwdriver or something that would suffice to remove the knob and access the locking mechanism.

She coughed. The smell was getting stronger. Her eyes burned. Some sort of chemical had been activated on the other side of the door and was seeping into the room.

Aubrey removed her lab coat, twisted it and placed it at the base of the door. Her coughing grew worse. She was having a hard time getting a breath. When she moved to get up from where she'd placed the lab coat, Aubrey collapsed on the floor.

She fought to not lose consciousness though it felt like she was falling down a dark hole. Her eyelids were heavy, her muscles weighted.

A banging noise came from the other side of the door. Her mind could not fathom what the noise was. She tried to lift her head off the floor. More banging. Someone yelling.

Arms were around her then, Isaac holding her and telling her it was going to be all right. She still felt very far away as if she were floating. She looked into his eyes as he lifted her and carried her out into the open part of the lab where the air was not poisoned.

Isaac screamed for someone to call for an ambulance.

She must have blacked out. When she opened her eyes, Isaac was holding her hand, telling her it was okay, that they were on the way to the hospital. His eyes filled with tears.

"You've got to pull through for me, Aubrey," he said. He squeezed her fingers.

For you, Isaac.

She slipped in and out of consciousness. Always when she came to, Isaac was there. It hurt to breathe.

She woke up in the dark on a bed. She pulled the crisp sheet tighter around her. She was in a hospital, probably the ER. She could hear sounds outside the curtain that had been pulled around her bed. A soft rhythmic noise indicated that Isaac had fallen asleep sitting in a chair by her bed. How long had she been here?

She stared at the ceiling as a chill ran over her skin. Someone had come into the foundation and tried to kill her. Or someone who worked at the foundation had tried to kill her. There were plenty of dangerous chemicals in the lab that could have been used to poison her through airborne means. The average person wouldn't know which chemical to use, but a scientist would.

"Hey, you're awake." Isaac stood up and hovered over her bed. "How are you doing?"

There was something sweet about his smile. "Breathing hurts. It feels like someone scraped the insides of my lungs."

"Another couple of minutes inhaling those chemicals and you would have been dead." He grasped her hand and put his face close to hers. "I'm so glad that didn't happen."

"It's good you found me in time," she said.

"Once I found you, I had to get us out of there fast, or I would have passed out too." He touched her cheek with his knuckle and sat back down. "Are you hungry or thirsty? I can let the nurse know."

"Just a drink of water would be nice."

"I can get you that." Isaac rose to his feet and poured water from a carafe that sat on a rolling tray. He handed her the plastic cup as she struggled to sit up in the bed. He adjusted her pillow behind her.

Isaac was being very attentive. She took several sips of the water and handed it back to him.

"Ruby and Brandie are handling the questioning about what your coworkers noticed. Trying to find out if a stranger was wandering around."

"It would be hard for an outsider to not be noticed on that side of the foundation."

"I guess there were some repair guys in fixing the air-conditioning. The outside door was left ajar so they could move in and out to get what they needed from their truck."

"I assume that whatever chemical was dumped outside the door was something from the lab, not something brought in from outside."

"We gathered a sample. The forensics people will figure out what it was."

Aubrey lay back down. "Any sign of Emily?" Angst came into her voice as she spoke.

Isaac sat down in his chair. "Ruby's dog picked up the clearest trail. We think that Emily initially tried to flee on foot but then returned to make a phone call in the public side of the foundation. The trail ends in the parking lot. The dog would lose the scent if she got into a car."

"Emily's car keys are probably still in her desk. She

would have been noticed if she came back for them. I wonder who she called for help."

"Ruby and Brandie are going to stake out your sister's place for a while, see if she comes back there," said Isaac.

Despair rose up as Aubrey placed her hand on her forehead. "What is going on with Emily?"

He reached for her other hand and held it between his two hands. "We'll get as many resources on this as possible. Ruby and Brandie will meet us back at the hotel in a bit around dinnertime. If three dogs and three officers can't keep you safe, I don't know what can. The doctor thought he could release you once you woke up and he could have a look at you."

"Is it that late already?" She had been out nearly the whole day. "I guess there wasn't a chance for anyone to hike back up to the site where I was shot at to gather more evidence."

"We'll get it done. I now realize my priority is to keep you safe," said Isaac.

Aubrey turned her head so she could look at Isaac. So his sense of duty had shifted from heading up the investigation to protecting her. She had to admit that when she thought Brandie was going to guard her, she felt a sense of loss. Had something between them healed enough that she didn't mind being close to him? She dared not hope for more. Yet she found herself wondering if he knew the real reason for their breakup ten years ago, could things be different between them?

Isaac was probably being kind because she'd almost died. "Thank you, Isaac, I appreciate that." Maybe they could at least work together without all the tension between them.

"Brandie and Ruby are going to help with finding

Emily," he said. "If we can locate her, I think she might have some answers for us."

If they could find her before she ended up dead too. "All we know is that Emily dated the man who is now dead. What links the professional climber and the other two men together?"

"Jasmin may have come up with something by now. We've been so busy I haven't had time to check my texts or voice mail. When I have a free moment, I need to call the chief about an issue with the candidates, and I'll check in with Jasmin if she doesn't contact me."

"Brandie seems nice. What's going on with the candidates?"

"With four people vying for two slots, we think one of them is trying to eliminate the competition, do things that make the other candidates look like they can't do their job or try to harm them like what happened with Brandie," said Isaac.

A man moved the circular curtain and poked in his head. "I thought I heard voices. I'm Dr. Crockett. I'd like to take a moment to look you over."

"I'll give you some privacy." Isaac got up and left her bedside.

After the doctor did a quick exam and asked her some questions, he said he would sign her out. "Your lungs have been damaged by whatever chemical concoction you inhaled. Rest is the best thing to ensure recovery."

She got dressed. When she stepped out from behind the curtain, Isaac was waiting for her. He led her back to his K-9 vehicle where Freddy gave her an enthusiastic greeting. "Ruby and Brandie got rooms at the lodge and picked up some dinner. They'll be waiting for us."

She didn't need to ask if Emily had returned to her apartment. Isaac would have given that news up front.

"I thought the four of us could eat together. Brandie needs to sit in on the conference call with the other candidates, but Ruby and Pepper can keep you company." Isaac must have made the call to his chief while the doctor was checking her out.

"By keep me company you mean protect me from another attack," said Aubrey.

Isaac chuckled. "I guess the euphemistic language doesn't make it any less bad."

Isaac's laughter had always sounded like a song to her. Even under such trying circumstances, it was good to hear it.

When they arrived at the lodge, Brandie and Ruby were waiting for them in the lower-floor room they'd checked in to. The burgers and fries were from the same food truck they had been to before when their dinner had ended up on the ground.

Though Brandie seemed on the shy side, the banter between Ruby and Isaac indicated that they were close. Their interaction reminded Aubrey of how a big brother would be toward a sister. The dogs sat by the door watching their respective partners, a Lab, a beagle and a German shepherd all lined up and ready for the next command.

Isaac and Brandie excused themselves to head upstairs for the conference call, taking Freddy and Taz with them.

While Ruby locked the door and closed the curtains, Aubrey sat down in a plush chair.

"Feel free to turn on the television." Ruby had already removed her gun belt before dinner. She pulled the gun out of the holster and placed it on the nightstand by one of the beds.

"I'm not much of a TV watcher. I think I downloaded a book on my phone."

"If you don't mind, I'm going to grab a quick shower.

I'm sure you know the drill. Not to leave the room or answer the door."

"Don't worry. Unfortunately, I'm getting used to this."

Ruby trotted into the bathroom. Her dog, Pepper, still sat by the door. As she opened up her e-book, Aubrey felt an emptiness. She was getting used to having Isaac close. She found herself missing him.

Aubrey was sure Ruby knew how to do her job. But it was Isaac she wanted to be with right now. He seemed different, less guarded since the accident in the lab. There was no indication, though, that he was over the hurt she had caused all those years ago.

Isaac and Brandie sat in front of the laptop, waiting for the other candidates and the chief to sign in.

"I told the chief what happened to you today," said Isaac. "You'll have to summarize for the other candidates."

Brandie nodded. "Thank you for setting this up."

The chief's face appeared in a square, and a few seconds later, the other trainees were visible. Owen, Parker and Veronica. Veronica was Jasmin's sister. There had been some talk of nepotism early on among the candidates, but Veronica really had held her own through all the assessments. Veronica looked a great deal like her sister with the same pixie haircut. Blond Owen came on the screen and then the dark-haired Parker.

The chief spoke up first. "I know that the competition between the four of you for the two open slots on the team has been intense. What we are concerned about here today is that one of you may have acted in an unethical and even dangerous way to make the other candidates look bad or unprofessional. Veronica being delayed when her help was required and Owen letting a safe house be breached because of bad communication are serious issues. Today, though, Brandie nearly lost her life when she was pushed toward a van that was backing up. Brandie, do you want to explain what happened?"

Brandie rubbed her hands on her thighs, communicating nervousness. She looked to Isaac for reassurance. Revisiting a near-fatal accident was never easy. He nodded.

Brandie recounted the accident.

"Did you see who pushed you?" asked Owen.

Brandie shook her head. "It was really crowded in the parking lot. I felt the weight and force on my back."

"Are you sure you just didn't stumble or trip over the leash?" Parker's question came across as condescending.

"Brandie took a pretty good tumble. I'd say she was pushed," said Isaac.

Veronica leaned closer to the screen as concern etched across her face. "Are you okay, Brandie?"

"Just got a little scraped up is all." She held up her hands. "Taz was pretty upset."

"Here's the thing," said Isaac. He retrieved the bugged napkin from one of his pockets. "We found this close to where Brandie was pushed. Or I should say Freddy found it." Everyone present knew that dogs will sometimes alert on something with a smell they have smelled before. Just as Freddy had done in Emily's apartment. He held the napkin close to the screen.

"Olympic Bed and Breakfast," said Owen. "Isn't that where you're staying right now, Parker?"

Parker wiggled in his seat and shook his head. "Hey now, wait a minute. Are you saying I drove all the way over to Mount St. Helens so I could push Brandie into traffic?"

"Can you account for all your time today?" asked Isaac.

Parker's voice dropped half an octave. "Not all of it. There was a huge chunk of time in the middle of the day when I was helping on a search and was alone in the forest." Parker bit his lower lip and let out a heavy breath. "Look, anyone could have dropped that napkin to frame me." Parker's speech had become staccato as he grew more agitated. "I don't like the way everyone is pointing the finger at me."

The chief was choosing to remain quiet, maybe gauging everyone's reaction. Isaac thought that was a good strategy.

"You are the only one who hasn't been made to look bad at this point," said Veronica.

"I know I got off on the wrong foot when this whole thing started. All I could think about was winning one of those slots. Being with this team working with these fantastic dogs has changed me. Finding God has made me want to be a better person. I get that I can come across as kind of stuck-up. I still want to be a K-9 handler with the PNK9 unit more than anything. But I wouldn't hurt Brandie or anyone else to get that." Parker's voice faltered. "You have to believe me."

No one else said anything.

"I don't think I'm being treated fairly," said Parker. "Most of the team has given Mara Gilmore the benefit of the doubt. I think I deserve the same courtesy."

"Parker is right that anyone could have dropped that napkin," Brandie said.

Isaac wondered if all the candidates would have been working close enough to the lodge in Olympic National Park to have grabbed the napkin. Including Brandie at some point. He'd take it up with the chief later.

"Parker," said Veronica, "I'm sorry if you feel attacked. We're police officers. What we should focus on is evidence."

"I'm not sure what to say," said Owen.

"I think Parker is right about giving him the benefit of the doubt," said Isaac. "We'll have to look into this some more."

"I agree," said the chief. "We will be back in touch. If you'll excuse me, I have a fundraiser I have to get to."

One by one the other candidates signed off.

"That was awkward." Brandie rose to her feet.

"A lot of tension there," said Isaac. "We'll get this resolved, just not right away."

"Thank you for setting everything up," Brandie said. "Even with the accident, I had a good day working with you and Ruby and staking out Emily's place."

In his brief interactions with Brandie, this was the first time she had seemed open to conversation.

"Ruby and I talked about a lot of things while we sat outside that apartment building," Brandie continued. "She's pretty upset about Eli Ballard being a suspect. I think she's going to try to find a way to cut things off with Eli without making him suspicious that the team is onto him."

"I kind of wondered. She got real quiet the other day on the video call when Eli being a suspect came up." Isaac rose to his feet and stretched.

"I agree with what Parker said. This is a great team. You support each other in your work and your personal lives," said Brandie.

She seemed to be hinting at something. "We'd do the same for any one of the candidates. Is there something on your mind?"

Brandie sat down in a chair, took a breath and looked at him. "I have a very personal reason why I wanted this assignment to work in the national parks. I talked a little bit about it to Ruby today. She said I should tell you too."

"I'm listening," said Isaac.

Brandie looked off to the side. Taz rose from where he had been resting and licked her hand. She stroked his head. "I think I may have been kidnapped as a child."

Though what Brandie had said was shocking, Isaac kept his response calm. It had probably been hard for her to reveal such a secret. "What makes you think that?"

"My parents, the people who raised me anyway, lived a really strange lifestyle, always moving, never really connecting with a community or neighbors. I had a feeling of not belonging even in my family as I was growing up. I didn't look like either of my parents. After they died, I found brochures of national parks in Washington from over twenty years ago. We must have visited them. I would have been three or four." She jerked to her feet and paced. "Here's the thing, and I hope this doesn't sound weird."

"Go ahead," said Isaac.

"As a child, I had these flashes of memory—at least I thought they were memories—of being surrounded by trees or next to a river. Since I have been in the parks, I realized that the people who raised me were never in the memory." She sat back down, shaking her head. "I might just be making this whole thing up."

"You know, there is a very practical way to look into your theory," Isaac said. "With Jasmin's help, we can access the cold case kidnappings that took place in the parks around the time you think it happened."

"You believe me," said Brandie.

"Why wouldn't I? It sounds like this is something that has followed you your whole life," said Isaac. "I think you should tell the rest of the team. We'll support you."

"Ruby said the same thing. Even if I don't get one of the spots on the team, working with everyone on the PNK9 unit has been a genuine pleasure."

"I'm glad I got to know you too." Though he couldn't say it, Isaac thought that Brandie deserved a spot on the team. Her initial aloofness now made sense.

Brandie's eyes teared up. "There's one more thing. Sometimes when I have dreams about being in the park, there's a little boy. I never see his face, just see him from the back. I think he's calling for me, but I can't hear what name he's saying. It's like he's just out of my reach. I don't know if it means anything. If memories and dreams can get all mixed up. It just seems so real."

Isaac handed Brandie a tissue. "That must be a pretty powerful dream if it causes you to cry to talk about it."

"Yes, but is it a dream or some fragment of a memory, something that really happened?"

"Hard to say." Isaac put his hands in his pockets and stared out the window. "Just know that we're glad to help you with the investigative part of your search for answers." He stared down at the parking lot and then out on the street.

There were new cars coming and going every day. No way to tell if the lodge was being watched. "I'm going to go get Aubrey and escort her up here. I will need you and Ruby to do guard shifts outside the room. Notify me if there is any strange activity in the parking lot or the trees at the back of the hotel."

"I can take the first shift. I'll go with you," said Brandie. Once they were down the stairs, they walked across the courtyard. "So is Aubrey the woman who broke your engagement years ago?"

"Has the team been talking about that?"

"Not in a gossipy way. I think they appreciate your professionalism under such difficult circumstances. Ruby and I were just worried about how you were doing emotionally."

He stopped staring out at the setting sun and gray sky. "My feelings are all over the place where Aubrey is concerned." His throat felt tight even talking about it. "Not sure what to think. Seeing her unconscious after she inhaled that chemical really wrecked me."

"Well, if you ever need to talk, both Ruby and I are in your corner," said Brandie. "You were a good sounding board for me, so I'd be glad to return the favor."

"Thanks for that. I hadn't realized how much I had been trying to deal with this on my own," said Isaac.

He knocked on the room where Ruby and Brandie would be staying. Ruby opened the door. When she stepped aside, he saw Aubrey from across the room. Her face brightened when she looked at him.

Isaac outlined the security plan for the evening. Starting at ten, Brandie would patrol the grounds and keep an eye on the door outside the suite. After four hours, Ruby would take over.

"Ready to go?" he asked.

Aubrey nodded, rose from her chair and crossed the room.

As Isaac and Freddy walked Aubrey back to the suite, Isaac prayed for a quiet night.

TEN

Aubrey awoke in the darkness to the sound of Freddy's intense barking. Still disoriented, she pulled the covers back and stumbled toward the light switch. She ran into the living room to find Isaac fully dressed and trying to calm Freddy.

"He never barks like that unless he's trying to tell me something." He pointed to the table across the room. "Hand me my phone."

She picked it up and brought it to him. Isaac was kneeling on the floor petting Freddy. "Brandie should still be on duty. Maybe she saw something." After a long moment, he pulled the phone away from his ear and stared at it. "She's not answering."

"Would Ruby already have taken her turn on patrol?"

He shook his head. "They each had a four-hour shift that started at ten. It's only one o'clock. If they changed the plan, they would have texted me."

Though Freddy was no longer barking, he still seemed upset.

Her mind scrambled for an explanation that didn't involve another attack. "Would he bark if Brandie had come up the stairs?"

"I don't know if she would do that unless she needed to warn us. She could watch the door and the stairs from below." Isaac pressed in more numbers. "I'm going to have to wake Ruby."

Feeling a rising tension while she listened to Isaac's phone call, Aubrey stood by the window that looked out on the forest.

"Hey, sorry to wake you…Brandie's not answering her phone and Freddy is agitated about something…Yes, that would be great if you and Pepper could have a look…I'll stay with Aubrey and wait to hear from you." He pressed a button on his phone and rose to his feet.

His face was etched with worry from the tight jawline to the crease between his brows.

"So much for a good night's sleep, huh?" She hoped her comment would lighten the moment.

Several minutes passed and Isaac stared at his phone. He pressed in a number. It must have rung several times. "Now Ruby's not answering her phone. Something's not right here."

"Maybe she's chasing someone and can't answer right now." Even that theory made her afraid.

"My gut instinct and Freddy's response are telling me we're under assault." He walked toward the door and then looked back at her as if trying to make up his mind. "We'll wait a few more minutes."

"I'll be all right if you need to go. I'll lock the door," said Aubrey. "It's important that you make sure the rest of the team is safe too."

He nodded. "Freddy will stay with you."

Isaac grabbed his gun belt and headed out the door. She walked across the floor to slide the dead bolt in place. She sat in a chair and stared at the floor, praying for everyone's safety. Freddy lay down at her feet.

After a few minutes, she rose and wandered to the window that looked out on the parking lot. With only one streetlamp working, it was pretty dark. Something moved at the edge of the lot and then disappeared behind a car.

She kept her eyes on the vehicle, watching for any movement. She was about to look away when she saw a flash of something reflective. It was too dark to see anything else.

Was her attacker out there?

She took a step back from the window and then turned off all the lights so no one could see inside. When she returned to the window, what she saw caused her to gasp. Taz was standing just outside the circle of illumination created by the single working streetlamp. He was alone and his leash dragged on the ground.

Not bothering to turn on the lights, Aubrey raced to her room. Her phone glowed on the nightstand. Her fingers trembled as she pressed Isaac's number.

"Yes." It sounded like Isaac was running.

"Something is really wrong," said Aubrey. "Taz is wandering the parking lot by himself. I wonder what happened to Brandie."

"Oh no." He didn't answer right away. She thought she heard footsteps. "I just found Ruby. She's been knocked unconscious. Pepper is still with her."

"Isaac?" They were still connected. She could hear thudding noises as if someone was moving around.

Aubrey's heart pounded. When she turned, Freddy sat protectively at the door leading into her room. Tension coiled around her torso making it hard to get a breath.

Something had happened to Brandie. Ruby was unconscious. Isaac was out there alone. He needed her help. Still holding the phone, she hurried up the dark hallway back into the living room.

"Isaac, if you can hear me, I'm coming to you. Where

are you?" In the dark, she ran into a piece of furniture. She cried out. Her phone fell out of her hand.

A breeze came from the window that faced the forest. Someone had opened the window.

A hand went over her mouth.

Freddy's rapid-fire bark filled the air.

She tried to swing free of the man who had grabbed her. She crashed into a table, knocking a lamp to the floor.

The door was dead bolted. Isaac would not be able to get in from the outside even if he had heard her.

Though he no longer had a hand over her mouth, the attacker had snaked an arm around her waist. The crook of his elbow pressed against her neck.

Freddy made growling noises. The man seemed to be shaking one of his legs. Freddy must have put his teeth into the man's pant leg.

"Get off me, you stupid mutt."

The distraction allowed Aubrey to get away. She pulled free with so much force that she landed on the floor. She crawled away toward the door then rose to her feet and ran.

Freddy yelped as though he had been kicked.

Her hand reached out, fumbling for the knob that opened the dead bolt. She twisted it. The attacker grabbed her from behind. While he held on to her shirt hem, she swung her body to face him. She lifted her hand to land a slap, but he punched her in the rib cage first. The blow knocked the wind out of Aubrey and disoriented her.

Again, she heard Freddy growling. It sounded like he was leaping up. If the little dog wasn't going to give up, neither was she.

The man had to have been dressed in black and wearing a mask. She could hear him as he fought off Freddy, who must have grabbed a sleeve. The white parts of Freddy's fur were visible.

If she ran to the door she could get away, but Freddy might end up hurt or worse. She felt around for something she could use as a weapon and found only the TV remote, which she threw toward where she thought the assailant might be.

A yelp told her she had hit her target.

"Come on, Freddy." She sprinted toward the door and flung it open. The man grabbed her and pulled her back inside.

He was breathing heavily as he turned her around and clamped his hands on her neck. Still squeezing her throat, he slammed her back against a wall. Pain radiated through her body.

She clawed at his gloved hands.

She couldn't hear Freddy anymore. Had something happened to the brave dog?

She gasped for air and grew light-headed.

Her hands reached for the man's collar and scratched his neck. She could feel herself about to pass out.

There was shouting and a clamor of noise coming from a distance. The pressure on her neck stopped and she was floating through space and then falling down down down. She saw a bright flashing light far away and then there was only darkness.

With Freddy at his heel, Isaac raced up the stairs to the suite. Freddy had found him as he tried to revive Ruby. He'd called for backup. The dog was frantically barking and rushing back toward the sidewalk and then back to Isaac. If Freddy had gotten out, something had happened to Aubrey.

The park police had just pulled into the lot when he

got to the top of the stairs. Some light from the parking lot spread into the room. Aubrey lay by the door on her side. He heard noise across the room. Someone was crawling out the open window.

When he ran over to the window, he saw a ladder, and a man running toward the forest. He returned to make sure Aubrey was okay. An officer appeared at the top of the stairs. It wasn't someone Isaac had dealt with before.

The officer shone his flashlight in the dark room. "What is going on here?"

"I'm taking care of her. The perp escaped out that window into the trees."

"On it." The officer disappeared.

Isaac gathered Aubrey into his arms. She was still breathing. He'd called an ambulance for Ruby, who had a bloody gash on her forehead. He still didn't know what had happened to Brandie.

He patted Aubrey's cheek. "Come back to me."

Freddy let out a whine and licked his muzzle, nudging Aubrey's arm with his nose.

Her eyes fluttered open. "Isaac. I was coming to help you."

"You should not have taken such a risk," said Isaac.

"After the way you protected me, how could I not come to your aid?"

Relief flooded through him. He touched her cheek lightly. "So glad you're okay."

Her eyes filled with fear. "He was here in this room. He came after me."

He took her into an embrace. "I know. I'm so sorry. We were set up. I never should have left you."

"Are Ruby and Brandie okay?"

"Ruby was injured." His voice intensified. "Not sure what happened to Brandie."

"I saw her dog in the parking lot." She touched his cheek. "You had no choice. You had to go help the members of your team." A tear streamed down her cheek. "Oh, Isaac, I was so afraid."

He held her, stroking her hair and making soothing sounds, finding a comfort in having her so close. The embrace eased his own fears. He pulled back to look her in the eyes. His finger traced a pattern on her forehead and down her temple. "I don't know what I would do if anything happened to you."

His lips found hers and he kissed her tenderly. She responded at first and then pulled away. Her eyes searched his. He kissed her on the forehead, rocking slightly as he held her. Her hand rested on his chest.

The kiss, however wonderful, had been impulsive, driven by a need to make her feel safe, to quell the fear that had engulfed her.

She released herself from his embrace and reached out to pet Freddy, who sat close to them. "If it wasn't for Freddy, things would have ended up much worse."

He was grateful when Ruby appeared in the doorway, breaking the awkward moment between them.

Ruby had a bandage on her forehead. "We found Brandie, or I should say Taz led us to her."

Isaac rose to his feet and held a hand out to help Aubrey up. "Is she okay?"

"I think she's fine physically. She was tied up and gagged," said Ruby. "Needless to say, she's been shaken up by the attack."

Ruby touched Aubrey's arm. "He came for you, didn't he?"

Aubrey nodded. "Freddy saved me."

Isaac took Aubrey in a sideways hug. "I need to get her checked out by the paramedic."

"Understood. Brandie is down there now."

Ruby turned and walked ahead of them down the stairs. Pepper sat at the bottom. Freddy took up the rear as they walked over to the ambulance.

Brandie was standing just outside the open ambulance doors holding Taz's leash. She came toward Isaac and Ruby. "I'm so sorry. I feel like I dropped the ball. He jumped me from behind. He had pepper spray to keep Taz away. I think Taz only got sprayed a little. He's sneezing but his eyes aren't watery."

"You handled yourself just fine, Brandie. This took us all by surprise," said Isaac. "Such a bold move."

Aubrey brushed his arm and stepped toward the ambulance. The sensation of her touch lingered as he remembered the kiss. He steeled himself against the renewed attraction he felt toward her. He'd been caught up in the moment. Fear over what might have happened to her had driven his action. He could think more clearly now. Opening his heart to her would just give her the chance to dump him. He wasn't about to live through that again.

One of the park police signaled that he wanted to talk to them. "I'll go talk to him," said Ruby. She trotted toward the officer.

Isaac turned toward Brandie. "Did you get a look at the guy?"

Brandie shook her head. "He was dressed in black and wore a ski mask on his face."

He suspected that Aubrey wouldn't be able to identify him either. They spoke for a few more minutes to see if Brandie could remember any more details. He didn't want to press too hard. The attack had to have been traumatizing, though Brandie seemed to be holding her own. The incident proved that Brandie did not fall apart in the face of violence.

Ruby walked back toward them just as Aubrey emerged from the ambulance.

"The park police have offered to post extra cars here for the rest of the night. It's too late to try to find another place to stay," said Ruby.

Isaac let out a heavy breath. His gaze moved toward Aubrey. How did she feel about that?

"Ruby is right," said Aubrey. "We'll be driving through the night to find a hotel. We all need sleep."

"The police are going to search the area until daybreak," said Ruby. "With such a large police presence, I don't think he'll feel comfortable coming back for round two."

"Okay," said Isaac. "But we're going to wake the night clerk and get moved to a different room."

"I'm going to go with the police to help with the search," said Ruby.

"No," said Isaac. "We need you here for extra protection. Brandie will need to get some sleep. Someone has got to stake out Emily's apartment tomorrow."

"You trust me to do that on my own?" Brandie shifted her weight from one foot to the other.

"Yes." Ruby and Isaac spoke in unison. Brandie, like the other candidates, was a K-9 officer with some experience under her belt. She'd proven herself to Isaac tonight with how she'd handled the attack.

"Besides, you won't be alone. Taz will be with you," said Isaac. "He should be recovered from the pepper spray by then."

Within minutes they had gotten another second-floor suite. Ruby left to patrol the grounds. Brandie took one room and Aubrey took the other. Isaac settled on the couch in the living room area. Freddy lay down at his feet. Isaac had pulled his gun from the holster and set it on the coffee table, ready for whatever else the night threw at him and his fellow officers.

ELEVEN

When Aubrey opened her eyes, the first thing she saw was Freddy sitting on the carpet staring at her.

He offered a couple of tail thumps when she looked at his round brown eyes.

From where she lay on her stomach, she reached her hand toward him. "Are you keeping watch over me?"

Freddy licked her hand. She got up. The beagle waited for her in the bedroom while she showered and dressed. When she entered the living room, Isaac was on the phone. He acknowledged her with a hand wave and pointed toward where the coffee maker was.

Seeing his face, the sparkle in his blue eyes, brought back the memory of the recent kiss and even the ones they had shared ten years ago. Though kissing Isaac felt like the most natural thing in the world, she knew there was too much that was unresolved between them.

She could only hear one side of the conversation, but it sounded like he was talking to Jasmin.

"Yeah, that hotel isn't too far from where we are," he said, "I'll go see what I can find out."

Isaac remained silent while Jasmin spoke on the other end of the line.

"Okay, let me know if you dig anything up on the other guy. I'll be in touch." Isaac ended the call.

She stirred sugar into her coffee and lifted the mug. "What's going on?"

"Brandie's watching your sister's place and working on finding us a more secure location to stay. Ruby is getting some much-needed sleep. She'll check out late. We need to take all our stuff with us and assume we'll be somewhere different tonight."

"I guess me going into work is out of the question."

"For now, you need to stay close to me. We are still low on manpower until my colleague Tanner can get here. After last night, I feel an urgency to move this case forward. Jasmin hit a snag with the man pictured outside the hotel from the photos on the thumb drive. Obviously, that is not his home. He must be from out of state."

"So how do we figure out who he is?" asked Aubrey.

"From the photos, we know what room number he stayed in or is staying in. You and I are going to go question the hotel staff and see if we can ferret out some information about him. Maybe he is still there. It's taking a chance for you to be out in the open, but staying here is not safe either now that the police presence is less. Besides, we need a break in this case before there's another attack."

"I think the important thing is that you are with me. I feel safe as long as you are close," said Aubrey.

"Thanks for saying that." The compliment made him smile. He lifted his phone. "Jasmin sent me an enhanced pic of the guy to show around."

Isaac didn't bring up what the kiss had meant, so she wouldn't either. As they made their way out to his vehicle, Isaac's demeanor seemed more guarded. She'd felt so close to him last night, but now the walls had gone back up.

They drove to the hotel where the third man pictured

on the thumb drive had stayed. Two three-story towers with a courtyard between them contained an abundance of flowers, trees and a fountain.

"Pretty swanky. Wonder what a room in this place goes for?" said Aubrey.

"Nothing I could afford," said Isaac.

She wondered what he meant by that comment. Isaac's family came from generations of money. "Really?"

He studied her. "After my parents died, I put my share of the inheritance into nonprofits. My brother oversees them. I live on my salary as a police officer."

The news surprised her and made her admire Isaac even more. "I had no idea." Maybe Isaac's mom had been all about wealth and appearance, but he certainly wasn't.

"Money can do a lot of good in this world, but it can also make you think you are special when you're not." He pushed open his door.

She wanted to ask him what experiences had led him to make such a dramatic change in his life, but he had turned away from her, with body language that suggested he didn't want to talk about things that had happened in the past.

She got out while he unloaded Freddy. "Stay close to me," he said. "As in don't leave my side."

They entered the hotel. Isaac approached the desk clerk, a dark-haired woman who was probably in her late forties. The woman's expression remained neutral as they stepped toward the counter, but she smiled when she saw Freddy.

"Excuse me," said Isaac. "We'd like to talk to you about a man who may still be staying here." He brought the photo up on the phone.

The woman studied it for a moment. "Yes, I remember seeing him around. He spoke with an accent and had a couple of guys following him around like they were his bodyguards."

Aubrey pressed closer to the counter. "What kind of an accent?"

The woman shrugged. "I'm not very good at discerning accents. I guess European but not English or Irish."

"We believe he was staying in room 314 and might still be?"

A man dressed in a white shirt and black pants who must have overheard the conversation stepped toward them. "He's not there anymore. I just helped a family transport their luggage to that room."

Isaac whirled around to face the bellman who seemed eager to talk. He showed him the photos. "Was it this man?"

The bellman nodded. "That was the guy."

"Can you tell me anything about him?"

"He was a big tipper, very imposing demeanor, like he was the boss of everything when he walked in a room. And I'd say his accent was more like Russian. He said he was in the States on business. When he was ready to check out, he didn't ask about the shuttle to the airport. The car I loaded the suitcases into was a rental. One of the guys he was with was studying a map on his phone."

"So you got the impression they were still going to stay in the area?"

The bellman nodded. "I thought I heard one of the guys he was with call him Dimitri."

Isaac turned back toward the woman at the counter. "Can you confirm the man's name?"

"I know he signed the guest registry. He checked in three days ago." She indicated a book at the end of the counter. "I have some business to take care of elsewhere." She walked away from the counter.

Isaac stepped toward the guest book.

The bellman wandered away as well.

Aubrey slipped in close to Isaac and scanned the signatures once he turned to the right page. "Good thing they wanted to cooperate."

"The uniform goes a long way in building trust."

"Plus Freddy kind of helped break the ice with the desk clerk." Aubrey smiled down at the dog.

Isaac glanced at his partner. "He has his charms. People who don't have anything to hide usually want to help the police."

Aubrey's shoulder pressed against Isaac's as she leaned close to study the signature page. The proximity made her heart beat faster.

"There." Isaac put his finger on a signature that was almost illegible. "What would you say that last name was?"

The only reason the first name even looked like Dimitri was because they had been looking for it. She leaned closer. "Stravinsky or Scholinsky. Maybe."

Isaac typed a note into his phone. "Or a variation of that. It gives Jasmin something to work with." They walked together toward the hotel entrance.

"Was she able to figure out who the other man was? The one who was jogging in the park and standing on that city street. That one didn't have an address, only the car."

Isaac held the door for her so she could walk outside. "You have a good memory."

She stepped out into the sunshine. "Maybe we should revisit those photos again."

Isaac offered her a soft smile. "Are we working on this together?"

The word *together* echoed through her brain. "If you don't mind. I'll die of boredom if I stare at the walls all day. Another set of eyes might be helpful."

"Let me call Jasmin with this information." He opened the back door of the K-9 vehicle so Freddy could jump in with a boost from Isaac.

Aubrey climbed into the passenger seat.

Isaac called Jasmin with the name they had come up with. "The last name might be a variation of Stravinsky. His handwriting wasn't terribly easy to decipher."

She glanced at Isaac as he reached to put the key in the ignition. She was willing to admit that she liked that they could get along as long as the past was a closed door. Being with him, helping him with his work, felt good.

"Do you know a place around here where we could have a little privacy and set up the laptop to look at those photos again? Your condo is close, isn't it?"

"Yes, my place isn't that far from here. I could make us some lunch. I'd like to grab some fresh clothes anyway."

"That would be private. No prying eyes looking over our shoulder while we review the files." Isaac pulled out on the road. "As long as I'm sure we're not being followed. If there's any chance we've brought trouble to your doorstep, we need to come up with an alternative plan."

They drove back to her condo. After Isaac grabbed his laptop, he and Freddy stayed close to her as she made her way up the walkway, put the key in the lock and pushed open the door.

When she stepped in and looked around, she felt like she'd been punched in the gut.

Isaac knew something was wrong the second he entered the condo. Aubrey let out a gasp as her hand fluttered to her mouth.

He stepped in beside her and pushed the door open even more. The place had clearly been tossed. Cushions from the couch were on the floor. Kitchen cupboards were flung open. Canisters had no lids. Every possible place a thumb drive might have been hidden had been searched. That had to be why this had happened. Maybe after their first hotel room had been searched, maybe before. He was sure he would find a similar scene in the bathroom and bedroom.

"I don't know why I expected anything different." Aubrey turned toward Isaac, and he wrapped his arm across her back. "He must have found out where I live pretty fast. It's clear I wouldn't have been safe here."

"We can't go inside. I'll notify the local police of a break-in and let them know it might be connected to a bigger case. Their crime scene people will pass any relevant evidence on to us."

He guided her back outside, taking the time to look at the lock to see if there was any sign of a break-in. Some scratches were visible on the metal. Could be evidence of lock picking.

Aubrey ran her hands through her hair. "My sister has a key." She shook her head as her gaze darted around. "I'm sorry I said that. It's important that I think the best of her, but I can't let go of the idea that she's gotten herself involved with some sinister people." Her voice faltered, indicating how upset she was.

Feeling protective of her, Isaac gathered her into his arms. He held her close, taking in the fragrant scent of her perfume. He glanced around at the quiet neighborhood. The attacker knew where Aubrey lived. There was a chance he had hired someone to watch the place just like he'd done with Emily's apartment. Or worse, that he was watching the place himself. "Come on, we should get back into the SUV."

"Can I at least grab some fresh clothes?" she said.

"Sure," he said.

He took in a deep breath once the three of them were secured in the vehicle. He made the call to the local police force, providing the K-9 unit's contact number if they came up with any fingerprints or other evidence.

After disconnecting from the call, he turned toward Aubrey, who still appeared agitated. Her fingers were laced together tightly, and her mouth formed a hard line.

He didn't have to ask her what she was thinking to know that she was ruminating on how violating the break-in was. Maybe if he could get her to focus on something else, he could pull her from her turmoil. "We are still faced with the problem of needing someplace private to look at those files again," he said.

"Maybe it would be better if we just stayed in your vehicle," she said.

"Sure, we can find a lot with some people around." He patted her leg.

"The library parking lot would have a few people, but it's tucked away and not visible from the street. We could park there," Aubrey said.

They waited for the crime scene people to show up before leaving.

After that, she gave him the directions, and they drove through residential streets to the library. Once he found a parking spot, he set up his laptop and opened the files. "Let's see if we can see what any of these photos might have in common. If we find something interesting, I can get Jasmin to enlarge and enhance." He clicked through Hans's file and Nathan's file. Nothing really stood out. Next was Emily's file.

He turned to face her. "Are you okay looking at this?"

Aubrey nodded. "My sister has a good heart. She has just had so many tough breaks. She protected and took care of me when we were first orphaned. Of all the people who should be on her side, it needs to be me. No matter what we find out."

Isaac clicked through the photographs.

Aubrey pointed. "Stop." She leaned closer to the screen. "The coffee shop that was clearly visible in Nathan's photo is here in Emily's, just on the edge."

"Could be. Do you recognize that coffee shop?"

Aubrey shook her head.

Isaac returned to the photos of Nathan Wharton where the coffee shop name was on the window. He googled the name and showed her the map that came up.

She shrank the map so it would reveal more streets. "I don't recognize any of the street names. I don't think it's close to where she lives."

He looked up Nathan's address, which appeared in the photos, and then pulled up a map that showed the coffee shop was not far from where he lived.

"That means my sister went to his neighborhood, maybe met him there for coffee."

"There's no time stamp on anything. Jasmin might figure out if there is one embedded. The timeline of when Emily started seeing Nathan might become important."

"You mean if she ends up going to trial for something."

"I didn't say that." He gave her a friendly elbow nudge. "I'm with you. Let's give your sister the benefit of the doubt. Innocent until proven otherwise. It is what the K-9 team has done with a new member who is suspected of a double homicide, and it's what one of the candidates asked for as well."

They went through the Russian man's photos and the other man who was as yet unidentified. Instead of focusing on the intended subject, Isaac studied the background in each photo. The businesses that surrounded him on the city streets and what was around him in the park where he had been photographed jogging. There was a placard that named the park as Beall Park. "Do you know where that is?"

Aubrey shook her head. "I'm sure it wouldn't be hard to figure out. What interests me is that other photo taken on the street."

Isaac clicked back to it.

Aubrey pointed. "There are a couple of businesses here. I can't read the signs though."

"Jasmin might be able to get more definition. She may have already started that process."

Isaac's phone rang. Jasmin. "What do you have for me?"

"I have an ID on the man who was at the hotel." Her voice sounded grim.

His stomach tightened. "That's good news, right?"

"Where are you at right now? I just got a notice from the locals about a break-in at Aubrey's home."

"We're at the library parking lot not too far from there. We're the ones who reported the break-in at her place. What can you tell me about this Dimitri guy?"

"Is there a newspaper stand outside the library?"

He looked through the windshield. "Yes."

"Why don't you go get today's newspaper, page five?"

"Okay. Why?"

"Because a picture is worth a thousand words," said Jasmin.

"Hang on while I go get one." He had a full view of Aubrey and the car while he walked the short distance to the newspaper stand. He returned to the car. He and Aubrey bent over the newspaper as he pushed the button so Aubrey could hear the conversation as well. "Jasmin, are you still there?"

"Still here, Isaac."

"Aubrey is here too. I've got you on speakerphone."

He turned to page five and scanned. A photo and short article caught his eye. The photo was of an official-looking head shot of Dimitri.

Aubrey gasped and sat back in her seat. The article said that Dimitri, a businessman from Russia, had been found dead in his hotel room.

TWELVE

Aubrey struggled to get a deep breath. Now three of the people from the thumb drive were dead.

Isaac gave her arm a reassuring pat before speaking into the phone. "Jasmin, I'll call you back. I think we better finish this conversation in a minute."

He closed his laptop. "Are you going to be okay?"

Freddy gave a supportive whimper.

She had the sensation of going numb. The news about Dimitri felt overwhelming.

Isaac brushed his knuckles over her cheek. His touch reconnected her with reality.

His blue eyes searched hers. "We should pray."

She nodded. He took her hands in his and prayed for Emily's safety as well as a resolution to the case and an end to the attacks on Aubrey. He closed the prayer with an *amen*.

She opened her eyes. They held hands for a moment longer, the warmth of his touch seeping into her skin and calming her. When they first met, they used to pray together all the time. She missed how it made her feel closer to God and to Isaac.

He let go of her fingers. "I need to call Jasmin back," he said. "I'll put her on speakerphone so you can hear the conversation."

She nodded and let out a breath.

He pressed in the number. "Jasmin, I'm back. Aubrey is here with me in the car. The article didn't say what the cause of death was."

"The guy died at ten o'clock last night. The coroner's report hasn't been released yet. For sure, they haven't had time for an autopsy if the COD isn't obvious. They must have notified his family if his name is in the paper. So they might know more than they told the press."

"This is the third guy off that thumb drive who has ended up dead. I'm not sure if we have that kind of time. Aubrey and I should go over to the hotel where he died and see if the staff knows anything about the cause of death."

"Wouldn't it be better if you stayed hidden? I might be able to make some calls. I know one of the forensic people from that county. I can see if I can get some details off-the-record before the official release."

"Were you able to find out how the other two men died?"

"Yes, Hans Hilstead was on a practice climb when a rope broke, and he fell."

"That sounds a little fishy. Professional climbers check their equipment all the time. But it could have been an accident. And what about Nathan Wharton?"

"A mugging that ended with him being stabbed," said Jasmin.

"Did they catch the mugger?"

"No, the police report said his wallet was missing, so they figured it was a robbery gone bad. It was in a part of town that isn't terribly safe."

"Three out of five people from that drive are dead. None of them looks like straightforward murder, but it can't just be coincidence that they're all on that drive," said Isaac.

"Aubrey, are you doing okay?" Jasmin's compassion was apparent even through the phone.

She appreciated that Jasmin was being sensitive to the fact that Emily might be marked for murder. "I'm holding it together thanks to Isaac's support. It helps to have Freddy here too."

Isaac shared Aubrey's theory that maybe enhancing the backgrounds in the photographs connected to the yet unidentified man might hint at where the photos were taken and why.

Jasmin said she would look at the background even closer than she already had and promised to get back to him as soon as she had any new information.

Isaac hung up.

"What now?"

It had begun to rain. Isaac turned on the windshield wipers and started the vehicle. "Let's go get some food before I eat my shoe. Drive-through would be the safest." He turned the key in the ignition. "You know what's around here. Any preferences?"

"There is a taco place about five blocks from here." Aubrey gave him the directions and he drove the short distance. They ordered the tacos and drinks. Isaac parked in the parking lot of the strip mall where the fast-food place was.

They ate with the rain coming down so hard that the view through the windows was murky and distorted. The food was not that tasty, but it filled a hole in her belly.

The smell had made Freddy sniff the air.

After he ate, Isaac checked in with Brandie. No one had returned to Emily's apartment. They talked for a moment longer.

From what she gathered from Isaac's side of the conversation, Brandie had found a new secure place for them to stay.

Isaac grabbed a piece of paper and a pen to write something down. He listened and wrote on the paper and then disconnected the call.

Aubrey shifted in her seat. "She found us a place to stay?" She took the last bite of her taco.

"Brandie said from how it looks from the online ads it should be pretty secure. She made an appointment for you and me to go over there and have a look. If it's workable, Ruby and Brandie will join us later in the day. Ruby should be waking up and doing a late checkout in a bit." He handed her the piece of paper with the address on it. "Do you know it?"

The paper said *Doris/Cottontail Cottage* and the address was listed. She shook her head. "No, I don't know any of the vacation homes around here."

"Brandie spoke to the woman who owns it. It's on some acreage that used to be a working farm. Assuming there are decent sight lines through the windows, if anyone came onto the property, we would have some warning."

Aubrey had never thought she would ever have to deal with something like sight lines to prevent being shot at. "If Brandie and Ruby are going to join us, won't the owner know something is up, especially if all the dogs and police vehicles are there?"

"Brandie thought the same thing and decided just to be up front with the lady. She told the owner that the K-9 team are protecting you while they work on a case. The place is more secure because it's out in the country. Not a lot of people driving by."

Isaac typed the address into the phone. They drove through the rain and out of town.

She listened to the windshield wipers swiping back and forth and wondered about Emily. Was she safe? Was she still alive?

Isaac turned onto some fenced property that had a long dirt driveway. The area was fairly flat, with a forest to the back of it but some distance away. Aubrey assumed the more stately house with a porch that ran the full length of the front belonged to the owner, and the square-looking building painted in pink, yellow and green was the cottage. The front yard had several old tractors on display that looked like they had been painted and restored.

As they approached, a blonde woman emerged from the big house and waved at them. She opened an umbrella and walked toward the cottage.

Isaac parked close to the structure. Leaving Freddy behind, they both got out of the car and made a run for the overhang of the porch where Doris waited for them.

Up close Aubrey estimated that Doris was in her seventies. The older woman had an infectious smile, and she kind of resembled the actress Doris Day.

"Where is your police dog?"

"We left him in the vehicle."

"I can't wait to meet him," said Doris. She pointed to the side of the house. "There are parking pads back there. The way the house is angled, your police cars won't be visible from the road. The officer who called about the place asked about that."

Doris put the key in the lock and opened the door. Aubrey stepped inside. The cottage looked like something out of a Beatrix Potter book. In fact, there were pictures on the walls that looked like scenes from the author's books.

"There are two bedrooms each with two beds, and of course the couch folds out."

Isaac walked around the living room and kitchen, looking out each of the windows, and then disappeared down the hallway. What a strange contrast to step into this fairy-tale world because her life was under threat.

Isaac returned a moment later. "I think this will work. Did Brandie set up a way for you to get paid?"

"Yes, we took care of all that, but she said you had the final vote on whether it would be a good fit. The kitchen is stocked with the basics. There is a little grocery store up the road about five miles. You probably passed it on your way in."

Aubrey assumed that Doris was referring to the gas station/convenience store they had passed. "I think I remember that."

Isaac pointed in the opposite direction than they had come in. "What's up the road that way?"

"Just two other farms," said Doris. "The road that goes by my house is the only way in and out." Doris excused herself and stepped outside.

Isaac glanced around. "It's kind of like being inside a dollhouse or something."

"It has its charm." Aubrey stepped toward the kitchen. "I can make us some coffee or tea. Whatever's available."

"Sure, that would be great. I'm going to go get Freddy."

Aubrey found the coffee maker and started a pot brewing. Through the kitchen window, she watched as Isaac walked Freddy. Isaac hunched in the rain, but it didn't seem to bother Freddy, who was sniffing the flowers and bushes that surrounded the cottage.

By the time the pair came inside, the coffee was ready. She brought a mug to Isaac after he took off his wet shoes. Freddy settled on the rug by the sofa, and she sat down opposite Isaac with her cup of coffee.

His phone rang. "Jasmin, what did you find out?... Okay, Ruby should be awake by now, I'll get her up to speed and send her over to the hotel." He disconnected from the call and then turned to face Aubrey.

She took a sip of her coffee. "I gather Jasmin couldn't find out anything about how the Russian man died."

Isaac nodded. "I'm going to brief Ruby on what has happened so far and see if she can go over to the other hotel, where Dimitri died, and talk to the staff there. Showing up in person worked for us at the first hotel. Maybe she will have the same good results we had." Isaac pressed the buttons on his phone.

As he talked, he wandered toward the back of the house, so she only heard the first part of the conversation.

Aubrey stared through the big front window at the long driveway and beyond. There was nothing she could do but wait and pray. She had no way to contact her sister. She'd already texted Mary to contact her if Emily showed up to work. She'd done everything she could.

The feeling of powerlessness was overwhelming.

As charming as the cottage was, it felt like a prison.

Isaac returned to the living room, where Aubrey sipped her coffee while she paced from kitchen to living room.

He understood her restlessness. He felt it too. While he knew he was the best person to provide protection for her, being sidelined from the action of the investigation was hard for him. Working the case would make him feel more like he was making justice happen.

He looked around the room. There was a bookcase that in addition to books contained a shelf that had board games on it. He pointed toward the stack of games. "It would pass the time."

She shrugged and walked over to where he stood. She pointed to a trivia game. "We used to play this one all the time with your little brother. Remember that?"

"Yeah, he loved it. Hugh was such a voracious reader he almost always won."

She locked him in her green-eyed gaze. "How is Hugh doing these days?"

Any mention of the past was riddled with potential land mines. "He dropped out of college when our parents died, but he's talking about going back." The tightening in his stomach signaled that he had some trepidation about bringing up the past.

"I always liked Hugh. He was a good kid, but I guess he's not a kid anymore." She looked him in the eye.

The butterflies in his stomach seemed to have calmed down. They could talk about some parts of their past; it just took both of them choosing not to be reactive. "I'm sure Hugh has fond memories of playing that game, as do I."

"Me too." She grabbed the box that contained the trivia game and handed it to him. "Why don't you set it up and I'll see if there is anything to snack on?"

He heard Aubrey opening and closing cupboards and then the sound of the microwave running. She returned with a large bowl of popcorn. Freddy rested at his feet on an area rug.

They had finished one game and eaten most of the popcorn when Isaac's phone rang. It was Ruby. "Ruby, I'm going to put you on speakerphone so Aubrey can hear this too. What did you find out?"

Ruby sounded breathless as though she were running.

"Just leaving the hotel. Some guy came to Emily's place. Brandie's tailing him. I'm going to see if I can help."

"Did you find anything out at the hotel about Dimitri?"

"The guy ordered a room service meal, and then he was found dead." The sound of a car door opening and dinging noises filtered through the phone. Pepper let out a single yip, probably picking up on Ruby's urgency.

"What are you saying?"

"I tracked down the hotel employee who found him dead. He said Dimitri's skin looked jaundiced."

Isaac sucked in air through his teeth. "Arsenic in his food maybe?" When he glanced at Aubrey, her face had drained of color.

The sound of a car starting to roll was in the background as Ruby talked. "Nothing official yet, just wanted to let you know. Look, I need to concentrate on my driving. I'll be in touch."

Before he even disconnected the call, Aubrey had risen to her feet and was pacing again. "For sure, the Russian man was murdered."

He moved toward her, and she fell into his embrace. He rubbed her back while she rested her head against his chest.

"I'm so afraid," she said.

He held her a moment longer, wishing there was something he could say to ease her fears.

She pulled free of the embrace and massaged her temples as though a headache was coming on. "The hardest part is just sitting here playing games that don't matter when my sister is obviously in real danger."

"I know. I prefer to be in the middle of the action too. But this is the safest place for you right now." He took her hand and ushered her back toward the bookshelf. "Let's pick out another game, or maybe there's a book you want to read."

"I know you're trying to distract me." She turned back toward the window. "Look, it's not raining anymore. Can we at least go for a walk? Or maybe we can go for a run together like we used to. I'm sure Freddy would like the exercise."

Being outside would leave them exposed, but they were miles from anywhere, and there had been no sign that they had been followed. "Okay, maybe a brisk walk with Freddy. Neither of us have the shoes for a run. Unless you have something in your overnight bag."

She shook her head. "A walk it is then."

The mention of the runs they used to take around the lake by his parents' house meant she was thinking about the things they used to do together and maybe even the love that had burned with such intensity. Playing the trivia game had opened up a door in a safe way to who they had been to each other years ago.

They stepped outside the back door, where there was a deck with some outdoor furniture. Freddy heeled by Isaac's side. He would let them know if he saw any danger.

Though there was no obvious trail, they walked toward the forest and the mountains in the distance.

When they returned to the cottage, rain was sprinkling out of the sky again. Isaac found a towel to dry off Freddy when his phone rang. Jasmin.

Aubrey came back into the living room from the bathroom where she had changed out of her damp clothes.

He hit the speakerphone icon. "Jasmin?"

"Look, I'm making your case a priority in terms of what I can do with a computer and a phone. I've had some interesting developments."

"Go ahead," said Isaac.

"We got legal permission to access Nathan Wharton's emails and phone content as well as Hans Hilstead's. Nothing much with Hans. He just wasn't big on written communication. But in one of Nathan's emails to a friend days before he died, he mentions he's going to *come into some money*."

"Interesting." Isaac turned to face Aubrey, who had moved toward him as she listened.

"It only took a few calls to track down who Hans mostly climbed and practiced with, and that guy said the same thing. That Hans talked of a big payday about to happen."

"That is the first thing that even begins to link them together," said Isaac.

"I don't know what it means. Probably they were involved in something illegal with the promise of a getting paid. The other thing I wanted to tell you is that I did figure out where the photos of our mystery man were taken based on the businesses in the background, after I enhanced them and I was able to get a partial read on a street sign. I narrowed it down to a street in Longview. I know you're just outside of Longview, so you're close. It's a business district not near anything residential."

"So maybe our mystery man works there." Isaac walked the floor while he talked.

"That was my thinking, judging from the way he's dressed in the photo. I'd say he was in finance or banking. Since you're on protection duty, I'm going to text Ruby with a list of three businesses on that street that might fit the bill."

"Ruby is not free right now. Aubrey and I will go. We have no choice if we want this investigation to move forward. The clock is ticking for finding Emily." Sitting around waiting wasn't doing either of them any good.

"Okay, it's your call. I'll text you the info. I doubt he works at a deli or a laundromat, which is also in that area. There are also several jewelry stores there. Maybe if the three businesses I've given you don't pan out, they might be a possibility."

"Okay, thanks. I'll let you know what we find out."

They loaded Freddy into his kennel in the back seat of the SUV and headed back to Longview. The drive took about twenty minutes to get to the downtown business district. Isaac left Freddy in the SUV.

The first business Jasmin had texted them was an investment firm on the second floor of the two-story brick building. No one at the firm recognized the man in the photographs.

Several buildings up the block, they entered a bank, which featured a lobby done in marble with an ornate copper ceiling. There was only one woman behind the long teller's counter. She looked up from her computer monitor. With Aubrey by his side, Isaac stepped toward her. In the quiet lobby, their footsteps echoed on the marble. The lack of visible employees or clients and the high-end decor suggested that this was not a bank where the average Joe deposited his paycheck, but that the clientele dealt in high caliber loans and business deals.

The teller smiled as they reached the counter. "Can I help you?"

"I'm wondering if you know who this man is." Isaac brought the first picture up on his phone, the one of the man dressed in a business suit.

The teller studied Isaac, who was in uniform. "Is this official police business?"

"Yes," said Isaac. "It's part of an ongoing investigation."

"That could be Michael, but it looks like it was taken from far away. Do you have another one where his face is clearer?"

He clicked to the picture of the man jogging in the park.

The teller's face brightened. "That's Michael Lumsford."

Isaac's heart skipped a beat. "He works here?"

"Yes, he does. Michael handles international transactions and loans for our overseas clients."

Maybe they would finally get somewhere. "Is he here right now? Could we talk to him?"

"Strangest thing just happened. Michael comes in from his late lunch with the newspaper to read. Something he always does, but a few minutes after he went into his office, he runs out saying he had something he needed to take care of."

"Do you know what it was about?"

The teller shook her head. "I will say I've never seen Michael that upset. He's a pretty even keel guy."

"I wonder if it was something he read in the newspaper," said Aubrey.

"I don't know. On his way out he set the newspaper down." The teller came from behind the counter and walked over to the kiosk where people wrote out their deposit slips. She handed Isaac the newspaper.

It was folded to the page that contained the story about the Russian man dying in the hotel.

Isaac's heart pounded. "How long ago did Michael leave?"

"Less than five minutes ago. He's got a bit of a walk to his car. Parking is such a bear around here, he usually parks in the underground garage. He drives a black Lexus." The teller pointed. "Take a left once you are outside. About four blocks away."

As he ran for the entrance, Isaac thanked the teller. Aubrey fell in beside him.

He only hoped they weren't too late to talk to Michael.

THIRTEEN

Even though her work kept her in good shape, Aubrey was breathless as she sprinted up the street keeping pace with Isaac. They saw the sign with the arrow for the parking garage and ran down the ramp.

It wasn't a huge parking garage. One floor, three rows of cars, six or seven deep.

Isaac called out Michael Lumsford's name. A car backed out of a space one row over. They ran in that direction. The car, a black Lexus, barreled up the ramp before they could stop it.

Isaac sprinted after the vehicle when it pulled out onto the street. He ran up the street trying to get the driver's attention.

A high-pitched sonic boom filled the air. The car zig-zagged and careened into a parked car. The noisy clang of car alarms filled the air. The few people on the street scattered; some slipped behind cars or into buildings.

As they ran toward Michael's wrecked car, Aubrey saw that the driver's-side window was shattered. Michael was slumped over the steering wheel.

"He was shot." Isaac glanced up as he gathered Aubrey into his arms and directed her toward the shelter of a parked car. More shots were fired. More glass shattered.

Sirens in the distance indicated that someone had

made an emergency call. The shooter must have been waiting for Michael to come out of the garage while on a building on the opposite side of the street. And now he had seen that Aubrey and Isaac had tracked Michael down. That meant they had an even bigger target on their backs.

Crouching, she pressed against the car while Isaac turned and peered above the trunk toward the two-story building across from the parking garage.

He turned back around and pressed closer to her. "I can't see the shooter."

With the police on the way, the sniper would probably not stick around.

"I need to check, but I think Michael Lumsford is dead." Glancing around, he walked over and reached into the car, then looked in her direction and shook his head.

Despair and fear battled within Aubrey as Isaac came back toward her. Another life was lost.

"I'm sure the police will have questions for us," he said. "We need to get back to that teller and find out what she knows. Stay low. Use the parked cars as cover just in case."

They made their way back up the sidewalk bent over and running. The teller had come outside on the sidewalk. Her hand was over her mouth, and she was shaking her head.

Isaac ushered her back inside the safety of the bank.

The teller tugged at the necklace she wore and ran her hands through her hair. "What is going on?"

"Michael is dead," said Isaac.

The teller's eyes grew wide. She shook her head even more intensely as her eyes rimmed with tears. "Did you have something to do with his death?"

"No, please believe me. I believe it's connected to

my investigation. I'm so sorry for your loss. It seems that you cared deeply about him, but a woman's life depends on us finding out how Michael fit into this case I'm working on."

The teller took in a ragged breath and nodded, calming down a little. "Okay."

Isaac walked over to where he'd tossed the newspaper and pointed to the Russian man's picture. "Did you see this man at all in the last few day? He's usually with two guys who function as bodyguards."

The teller shook her head.

"Have you been behind that counter for the last few days, so you would have seen who came and went from the bank?"

The teller nodded. "I'm here anytime the bank is open. I usually even eat my lunch at my desk." She pointed to a desk that would still allow her to see people come and go.

"There's no one else who would have seen who came and went through those doors?"

"Not likely. Everyone else is in an office most of the time." The teller tilted her head as if thinking. "Some of Michael's business dealings are done over lunch, which is more relaxed than his office. It's possible he met that man outside the bank."

"Did he share with you anything unusual going on in his professional or personal life?"

"Michael was a very private man. Other than talking about his golf game, he rarely said anything about what went on in his life," said the teller.

"What kind of business transactions was he working on? Did you handle any of the support paperwork for him?"

While Isaac continued his questions, Aubrey prayed they were not at a dead end. Judging from the photos, the killer had not known where Michael lived. He was photographed outside his place of work, so his connection to all this must be work related.

The teller shook her head but then stopped. "Wait. It didn't seem important at the time, but yesterday he said some offhand remark about difficult clients, having put in time on a deal that fell apart at the last minute. He was pretty upset about it."

"Do you remember what the deal was about?"

"Michael would never betray a client's privacy. One of the things he did was large money transfers from foreign countries. It might have been related to that."

"He didn't say which country? Russia maybe?" said Isaac.

"Michael worked with people from all over the world. He spoke four languages."

Through the glass walls, Aubrey saw two policemen standing outside. She tugged on Isaac's sleeve.

After answering questions for the police, they were given permission to leave.

When they got in the SUV Freddy wagged his tail from his kennel. Once he was settled behind the wheel, Isaac turned toward her. "You doing okay?"

She shook her head. "My sister is the only one left on that drive who may still be alive. We have to find out what happened to her."

"I know." He patted her leg.

Aubrey appreciated that he didn't tell her that everything was going to turn out okay or that they would locate Emily before it was too late. Isaac wouldn't say things that weren't true. This was in God's hands. They could not control outcomes, only work as hard as they could to resolve the investigation before it was too late.

As they sat with the parked car running, Isaac's attention was drawn to the roofs of the two-story buildings that surrounded them. "As a precaution, I'm not going directly back to the cottage. He knows we're onto him. We have to make sure we're not followed."

While Isaac drove through the town and then out into the country constantly checking his mirrors, she tried to piece together what Michael's death meant.

"Michael Lumsford must have seen the man who is behind all of this if he was doing some kind of deal with the Russian," said Aubrey.

"And the deal fell apart or the Russian didn't want to pay the asking price for whatever it was that was exchanging hands," said Isaac, "so the Russian died."

"It must relate back to Emily and the foundation and the other two dead men."

"Why was that thumb drive in such a remote place?" Isaac wondered out loud.

"I think it was dropped there by accident. The guy must have been up there for a different reason."

Isaac continued to drive around into the early evening. He spent some time on the phone getting Jasmin up-to-date on everything that had happened.

After grabbing some food from a drive-through, Isaac drove around eating small bites of food.

The stiffness of Isaac's posture indicated how aware he was of the possibility of an attack given what had happened to Michael.

She ate the Thai food and sipped her drink, not really tasting anything.

Isaac found a place to park on a tree-lined street and picked up his phone. "I need to call Ruby and get an update."

Ruby's voice came across the line. "We didn't catch the guy. I'm going to continue to stake out Emily's place. Brandie is headed back to our new digs for a quick shower and some rest before she takes over the stakeout in the a.m. hours. Maybe the guy will come back."

"Did Brandie get a look at the man who came to Emily's door?"

"She said he was tall and lean. She couldn't see his face. His back was turned toward her the whole time."

"Did he break into the place?"

"I'm not sure of the details. You'll have to ask Brandie when you see her."

"Okay, Ruby. You take care." He glanced at Aubrey. "On a personal level too. You know what I mean. Maybe we can talk later."

"Sure," said Ruby. Her voice sounded a little guarded.

It was clear Isaac wanted to protect his friend's privacy about personal matters. On the conference call Aubrey had noticed a change in Ruby when the possibility of a man named Eli being involved with something criminal had come up.

Isaac said goodbye and disconnected from the call. By the time he made the decision that it was safe to head back to the cottage, the sky had turned gray.

Once they turned onto the country road that led to the cottage, Aubrey found herself checking her side-view mirror as much as Isaac did. It would be easy enough to tell if someone was following them now when there were so few vehicles that had a reason to go this way once they were past the convenience store.

If they had been followed up to that point, the attacker would have blended in with the rest of the traffic.

No matter what, she couldn't let her guard down.

Isaac couldn't shake the heavy feeling he got as they pulled up to the little cottage. He was glad to see Brandie had parked her car so it wasn't visible from the road.

Aubrey had grown quiet, spending most of her time staring out the window.

She got out and headed toward the door. Isaac let Freddy out of the back of the vehicle and let him sniff around and pee before calling him in.

Brandie was inside. Her long brown hair was wet from a shower while she stood at the counter eating something out of a bowl.

"I know you need to get some shut-eye, but can you tell me exactly what happened with your encounter today? This is the first break we've had with what's going on with Emily."

Brandie put her spoon down. "The guy came around the back of the building. He must have parked one street over. I got out to confront him and he ran." Brandie stared at the counter. "Maybe I should have just hung back and watched him then tailed him anonymously."

"It's always a judgment call," said Isaac.

"I didn't even have time to deploy Taz. I think procedurally, I should have done things differently." Brandie took a bite of the chili she had in her bowl.

"Don't be so hard on yourself," said Isaac. "It's easy enough to do Monday-morning quarterbacking. The more experience you have, the better your in-the-moment decision-making will be."

"You're probably right." She rinsed her bowl and put it in the dishwasher. "Everyone has been so great and supportive. I wanted to let you know, at your suggestion, I shared with the rest of the team on the group text about believing I may have been abducted in one of the parks in Washington. The whole team pledged to help me in my search as much as they can. Jasmin is going to pull the cold case kidnappings from the parks that fit my timeline."

"That's good to hear," said Isaac. "I'm sure you want to get some answers."

"For sure." She suppressed a yawn. "I'm going to try to get some sleep before I give Ruby a break." She turned to face him. "I'll drive out and relieve her of stakeout duty, so she can come back here to sleep. That way there won't be a span of time when we don't have eyes on Emily's place."

"Good. Tell her she can have the bedroom you were in," Isaac said. "Aubrey can have the other one and I'm going to stay in the living room."

Brandie headed up the hallway to the bedroom with Taz trailing behind her.

Aubrey sat down on the couch. "Wow, that sounds like a lot for Brandie to deal with, being kidnapped as a kid."

"At least now, she's not alone in trying to find answers."

She let out a heavy sigh and moved the pieces of the trivia game around mindlessly. "I know how she feels having such a heavy emotional thing to deal with."

He took a seat close to her and wrapped his arm around her back and pulled her close. She melted against him, resting her head on his shoulder. "I know you're worried about Emily."

"How does any of this make sense? Five seemingly unconnected lives. Four of them dead." Her voice faltered.

He pulled free of the sideways hug. "Not totally unconnected. We know that Michael was upset when he saw that Dimitri had died. We can assume that Michael had interacted with him, probably as part of his work. Michael was probably also killed because he had seen the man who is behind all this. We know that your sister knew Nathan Wharton well enough to have dinner with him."

"The fact that she put that picture of them together as a wallpaper on her phone suggests they were romantically involved," Aubrey said.

"We don't know what Hans Hilstead has to do with all this. We only know he and Nathan thought they were going to come into some money," said Isaac.

She ran her fingers through her long blond hair. "I'm tired of trying to figure this out, and I am still too wound up to go to sleep."

"Looks like Doris has a nice movie selection." Isaac rose to his feet. Aubrey's taste had always run toward nature documentaries when they were dating. He didn't see anything that fit the bill. Instead, he pulled out an animated movie that might provide some levity and free her from worrying about her sister.

She nodded. "Sure, put it on." She moved toward the kitchen. "I think I saw some flavored water in the fridge. You want one?"

Even after they sat down to watch the movie, Isaac sensed Aubrey's unsettled state of mind. She stared at the screen as if she wasn't really connecting with the story.

The movie wasn't finished when she rose and said, "I think I'll try to get some sleep."

"Freddy and I will keep watch out here." He pointed toward the big front windows that provided a view of the road.

Aubrey said good-night.

Isaac let the movie run until the end though he paid little attention to it. He turned out all but one light and lay down on the couch. He closed his eyes and rested, knowing that Freddy would alert him if anything were amiss.

He was awakened a few hours later by Freddy's single yip. He heard the back door open and close, and then

Brandie's K-9 vehicle started up. She'd probably used the back door out of consideration so as not to wake him.

He was still half awake when about forty-five minutes later, Ruby's K-9 vehicle rolled up the drive and parked by the side of the house. Brandie must have given her the heads-up about where to park. She used the back door as well. Being this far out in the country meant they were putting in a lot of miles to get to the places connected to the investigation.

He fell back asleep but jerked awake maybe an hour later as a realization hit him. A PI had been hired to watch Emily's place. What if whoever was behind these crimes had found another PI to do the same? He could have followed Ruby here and let his client know where they were hiding out. He thought they had covered all the bases, but maybe not.

That didn't explain who the man was who had shown up at Emily's place or why.

What made the most sense was not to stay here too long. They'd have to find another location for Aubrey to stay tomorrow.

He drifted back off to sleep but woke when he heard Freddy growl. He sat up, waiting for his eyes to adjust to the darkness. The dog had put his front paws on the window that faced the road.

He didn't see anything but shadows outside, but something had caused Freddy to be alarmed. He watched through the window.

The beagle growled again. Something was out there that made Freddy nervous. It could be a bear or coyote… or a human being.

Freddy dropped down to the floor from the windowsill but still paced.

Isaac remained still, not wanting to call attention to

himself if what was out there meant them harm. As his eyes adjusted to the darkness, he was able to separate out some of the shadows. All of Doris's windows but one were dark. He could see distinct trees that lined the driveway leading to the cottage.

His heart pounded as he waited and watched. Freddy stood by the door and growled. He'd trust his partner's instinct over his own any day. Freddy was communicating that he sensed a threat.

A minute passed and Isaac rose to his feet. He retreated to the kitchen and looked out a window that provided a view of the side of the cottage. Something was moving by the bushes that were a few feet from the house.

Freddy let out three quick barks.

Isaac ran back to the living room where he'd taken off his gun belt. He hurried down the hallway and roused Ruby. "Get your gun. We have a prowler. I don't know if it's animal or human." Pepper, who slept on the floor by the bed, woke up ready for duty.

Ruby gave a mumbled response but reached for her gun belt.

"You take the back door. I'll take the front," said Isaac.

He hurried back to the living room, commanded Freddy to follow and opened the door to the night. Just as he stepped outside, he heard the back door open and close. He lifted the flashlight from his belt and shone it around the area where the two cars were parked.

Freddy remained close as they patrolled the front yard and then turned toward the hedge on the side of the house where he had seen movement. He shone the light through the leaves. Freddy stayed close to him.

Pepper barked from the other side of the house. Ruby must have cleared the back by the deck and come around to meet him in front.

He turned back around to see Ruby and Pepper approaching.

"Something got Pepper agitated as we came around to the front of the house," said Ruby.

Lifting his flashlight, Isaac did a slow arc around the yard.

Pepper let out a low growl.

"Did you see that?" Ruby was pointing up the road.

"What?"

"Lights flashing on and off. Super quick."

"Two lights?"

"Yes, like headlights. Someone not wanting to be seen but needed to figure out where the road was."

"Shh…listen," said Isaac. Though it was not distinct, he thought he heard the soft hum of a car engine. Whoever had come here had parked at the end of the long driveway.

The dogs had certainly indicated that a threat had been present. Perhaps the assailant had weighed the odds and realized an attack was not a good idea.

"Is everything all right?" Aubrey had come out on the porch, crossing her arms against the night chill.

"We got it under control. Let's go back inside." Isaac and Ruby followed Aubrey into the living room. "I don't think we should stay here any longer. Let's get packed up and head out."

"I'll notify Brandie about our change of plans." Ruby spoke as she headed down the hallway.

"You said things were under control." Fear permeated Aubrey's voice.

The dogs had thwarted another attack, but the culprit knew where they were staying and now he had time to plan. This might even have been a reconnaissance mission, since the attacks all seemed to have a level of planning.

"We just can't take any chances, Aubrey," said Isaac.

"I'll throw my stuff together." A tone of resignation filled her words.

Within minutes, they were loaded up and rolling along the long dirt driveway. Isaac's SUV was in front, and Ruby took up the rear, driving through the night.

Isaac was resigned to the fact that there was no truly secure place for Aubrey. All they could do was provide protection and remain vigilant.

FOURTEEN

As they drove on the dark country road, Aubrey took note of Isaac's silence. It was out of character for him to not be encouraging and positive. The look on his face was pensive, his mouth drawn into a tight line. Did he feel as defeated as she did?

Once the country road connected with the highway, he seemed to be focused on the traffic around him. Though not many cars were on the road at this hour, his spine stiffened every time one slipped in between his car and Ruby's.

"You probably didn't get much sleep." She hoped to sound supportive.

"This line of work, a person gets used to it," he said.

"All the same, I'm sure you could use a solid block of rest. We still have hours before daylight."

"What are you saying?"

"I saw a billboard for a pet-friendly motel at the next exit. We all could use more sleep," she said.

"As long as I'm certain we're not being followed. Ruby was pretty sure she saw a set of headlights right where the driveway meets the road."

"Oh, I didn't realize." She tugged on her scat belt where it dug into her skin.

"I didn't want you to worry any more than you already are," he said.

He took the exit that had advertised the pet-friendly motel but did not drive directly there. He pulled over. "What was the name of the motel? The sign went by in a flash." He'd picked up his phone.

Ruby pulled in behind them on the quiet residential street.

Aubrey recited the name of the motel. Isaac stared at his phone, waiting for the directions to come up.

Ruby's voice came over the radio. "What's the plan?"

Isaac pushed the talk button on his radio. "Gonna try to find a place to bunk for the rest of the night since we all could use the sleep. Follow me, give me a heads-up if you have any indication we're being tailed."

"Ten-four," said Ruby.

They drove through the small tourist town. The white stucco of the motel was visible in the moonlight. After rousing the night clerk, they got adjoining rooms, both with two queen beds in them. The rooms were clean but outdated with a decor that looked like something from the eighties.

"Why don't you get some sleep, Isaac? The bags under your eyes are bigger than the ones under mine," Ruby joked.

"If you're okay with that?" Isaac's gaze locked on to Aubrey.

"Sure. You're not a superhero. You need to sleep." It warmed her heart that his first thought was of her.

"Wake me in a few. Ruby, if you could text Brandie and let her know where we relocated to." Isaac retreated to the other room with Freddy, leaving the door slightly ajar.

Aubrey lay down on one of the queen beds without

bothering to get under the covers. Ruby took up a post in a chair that looked out on the quiet street. She removed her gun belt, pulling the pistol from the holster and placing it on the windowsill, probably so she could grab it quickly if she had to. Pepper took up a position by the door. Though the black Lab lay down, it was clear from the way she held her head up that she was still on duty.

Aubrey closed her eyes and fell into a restless sleep filled with dreams about running and being chased. Sometime in the night someone draped a blanket over her.

She awoke to the warmth of sunlight streaming through a window and the smell of coffee. When she rolled over, Isaac sat in the chair by the window sipping coffee from a paper cup. He pointed to the coffeepot. She nodded.

Isaac seemed to indicate they needed to be quiet. The door between the two rooms was shut, so either Brandie or Ruby must be asleep in the next room.

Aubrey got up and went into the bathroom to freshen up. When she returned, Isaac handed her a steaming cup of coffee.

Isaac spoke in a low voice. "We've got another PNK9 officer coming today to help out with the investigation. Tanner Ford and his boxer, Britta, are on their way. Ruby is taking a power nap. Brandie is still watching Emily's place. Once Ruby wakes up, she's going back over to the bank where Michael Lumsford worked and try to get more details. If he had a business lunch with the Russian man and whoever was trying to broker the money transfer, maybe the waitstaff remembers him. We can get a clearer description and maybe a better idea of why so much money was changing hands."

"And what are we doing? Just hanging out here in exile until we're found again?" She caught herself. "Sorry that sounded really bitter. I appreciate the sacrifices that have been made on my behalf."

"It's all right. Finish up your coffee."

Before Aubrey took the last sip of coffee, Ruby poked her head in the door. "Pepper and I are off to see what we can dig up about what Michael Lumsford knew that got him killed."

"Hope we get some answers as to what the man at the lunch looked like," said Isaac. "And Ruby, I know you got a lot on your mind. You've been a true pro all the same."

"Thanks," said Ruby. "Maybe we'll get a chance to talk once this all quiets down."

"For sure," said Isaac.

Ruby and Pepper left the motel room.

Isaac's phone rang. He looked at the call screen. "It's one of the park officers." He clicked the connect button. "Officer Lansbury, what's going on?"

Aubrey was able to hear both sides of the call.

"Sorry to be so slow in getting back to you. Nielson and I have been busier than a cat in a room full of rocking chairs. Summer not only has more tourists, but more crime. Anyway, we did come up with a usable print from that smear on the glass in the basement."

Isaac shifted his weight. "Did you run it through the system?"

"Yup and we came up with a name. Turns out the guy had a record. Nathan Wharton."

Aubrey's breath caught as Isaac's gaze met hers.

Lansbury's voice came across the line. "Does the name mean anything to you?"

"Yes, it does actually. It would take a moment to get you and Nielson up to speed. I can tell you that Nathan Wharton died under questionable circumstances, and we believe he is somehow connected to the attacks on Aubrey Smith."

"Nielson and I are headed back over to the foundation. One of the scientists, Christopher Brink, seemed to think other things were amiss in the basement. We're going to have a closer look. You're welcome to join us. Maybe we need to swap some notes if this is more than a simple break-in."

Isaac glanced over at Aubrey as if questioning if she was okay with returning to the foundation. She nodded. Anything was better than sitting in this motel room.

"I'm on my way," said Isaac. After loading up Freddy, he and Aubrey got into the SUV. He turned to face Aubrey. "You need to stay close to me while we're out in the open."

"Only the researchers and support staff are on that side of the foundation. You can only go into the public side from the foundation, not the other way around."

"I don't want to take risks where you're concerned." His voice intensified. "But if there's something I can do to connect the dots on this case, I have to do it, so you can be safe in the long run."

She could hear the angst in his voice. If they could catch who was behind the attacks on her, she would no longer be in danger. "I know that you would do everything in your power to keep me safe. We haven't been any less vulnerable in these hotels. Might as well try to get something done."

"Point taken," said Isaac. He started the car and shifted into Drive. He hit the blinker and turned on the road that led to the foundation. Officer Nielson was waiting outside when they pulled into the employee parking lot, which was nearly full of cars. So full, that Aubrey wondered if some tourists had parked on this side when the public lot was full despite the posted signs. Something about the full parking lot bothered her.

Officer Nielson ushered them both inside along with Freddy. "We got a full forensics team in the basement this time. There are prints all over the place so once we lift them, it will take time to sort through them. All the employees have agreed to be printed."

Isaac looked at Aubrey. "What's in the basement anyway?"

"The old lab that is hardly ever used, and I think some files are stored down there. Duncan would know." He made a point of letting everyone know that he was the senior researcher and had been with the foundation longer than Leandra.

Aubrey moved toward Duncan's office but found it locked.

Mary, the receptionist, had come out from behind her desk. "Duncan didn't come in today, and he didn't call in with an explanation."

Aubrey felt light-headed, as if she had just put headphones on. It seemed like there was a connection she needed to make but couldn't quite put together. "He didn't say anything to Christopher or Leandra about where he would be working?"

"No, I asked them if they knew." Mary shook her head. "You know Duncan. He kind of does his own thing. He can get absent-minded about common courtesies when he is in deep research mode. He didn't pick up when I called his landline or his cell."

Mary was right about Duncan not feeling like he needed to communicate with the rest of the researchers. "I suppose he could be at home doing something on his computer and just doesn't want to be interrupted."

"Must be. He didn't sign out to be in the field," said Mary.

"Do you know what is down in that basement?"

"I just always assumed it was storage. One of the rooms requires signing out a special key card that Leandra keeps. Not sure why."

Maybe Duncan had simply not wanted to communicate the reason for his absence, but she wondered if his conversation with Emily yesterday was connected to his aloof behavior. "Did Duncan sign out for that key recently?"

"I can go check." Mary returned to the counter where her computer and foundation phone were. Her head disappeared from view while she pulled out a clipboard and glanced at it. "No one has been down there in over ten months, not since I was hired."

Isaac had wandered away from his conversation with the other officers and was listening to Aubrey and Mary.

"If the room has the extra security of sign-out and a special key card, it must be more valuable than old equipment." Isaac put his hand on her shoulder. "The forensic team might want to have a look. Why don't you get that key card?"

Aubrey signed the sheet that Mary produced. She didn't even recognize the name of the person who had signed out previously. It looked like the room was accessed maybe once or twice a year. Once she signed the sheet, she took it and showed it to Leandra, who gave her the key card. "Do you know what's in that room?"

Leandra said, "I've only been in there once. It looks like a bunch of PhD dissertations, records of previous research. You know how scientists feel about their work. It's so valuable, it must be put under lock and key. A lot of the research down there is so old it hasn't even been cataloged in our system, and it's probably outdated."

Like all scientists, volcanologists built their ideas on

previous research. A dissertation usually required a section outlining previous related studies. Maybe that was why the old research was kept.

Leandra took a sip of her coffee. "I keep thinking we should go through there and get a better idea of what is worth uploading to a digital database, but it just hasn't happened with everything else that has to be done."

Aubrey knew that the more recent research had already been cataloged and made available to other places that studied volcanos, so whatever was down there was old. Aubrey walked back over to where Isaac was waiting.

She waved the key card.

When Aubrey, Isaac and Freddy arrived downstairs, Nielson and Lansbury were waiting while the fingerprint tech, a short woman with gray hair and glasses, continued to dust, lift and store prints on and around the doorknob.

"This is going to take forever to sort," said the tech.

There were two doors on either side of the hallway. Christopher had left some boxes in the hallway the night he said there was a break-in. He thought they had been bumped into or kicked. She knew the room without the key card contained samples they thought they might need as well as being a catchall room for things they weren't currently using on projects but thought they might need. Also, past educational materials from when they gave lectures to the public were put in the unlocked room.

Once the tech was done with the outside of the door, Aubrey sliced the key card across the scanner and pushed the door open, wondering what they'd find inside.

The first thing Isaac smelled when Aubrey opened the door was dust. The air was stagnant with it.

The tech stepped into the room. "Now if someone

had recently been in here, finding a fingerprint might be a little easier."

Isaac stepped inside and switched on a light. Aubrey, Lansbury and Nielson followed. Freddy sniffed and then swung his head from side to side. He made a noise to get Isaac's attention. Some scent in this room was familiar to Freddy.

There seemed to be a fine layer of dust on everything. There were file cabinets and shelves with stacks of bound papers as well as film, VHS and DVDs.

The tech had taken out her flashlight and was studying the file cabinets and shelves very carefully. "A fresh print would show up pretty readily with this layer of dust."

Aubrey took one of the bound piles of paper from a shelf. It was a 1999 PhD project from a scientist whose name she didn't recognize. "I think this is where old research goes to die."

Christopher came to the open door. "What's going on here?"

"We think this room might have been broken into. Do you know of any research that would have been valuable enough to steal?"

Christopher started to shake his head and then stopped. "I do remember Duncan talking about simulations being done to make a volcano erupt on purpose."

Aubrey's voice faltered. "Was that…Duncan's research project?"

Christopher shrugged. "I don't know who the researchers were. Duncan mentioned it in passing. I think the idea was that doing small eruptions on purpose could prevent the buildup of pressure that would cause a big explosion. I need to get back upstairs." Christopher disappeared.

"Still, that could be dangerous in the wrong hands."

Aubrey was visibly shaken by what Christopher had said. Isaac brushed her arm hoping to calm her.

The tech stopped at a shelf at the back of the room and began to dust in several places.

"If she can lift a decent print, it won't take long at all to see if it matches Nathan Wharton, which would confirm that he was in here," said Lansbury.

Light sparked in Aubrey's eyes. She tugged on Isaac's sleeve. "I know now what was bothering me earlier. We need to go back upstairs."

Nielson assured Isaac they would let him know if there were any developments. Aubrey hurried up the stairs so fast that Isaac and Freddy had to trot to keep up with her. She pushed open the door and stepped out into the parking lot.

She was only feet away from the metal sculpture where she had been shot at. Isaac moved toward her. "Maybe we should go back inside."

She ran through the rows of cars, calling back to him. "Emily's car is not here anymore. There were so many extra cars here when we pulled up, it didn't register with me at first."

Isaac and Freddy reached her side. Aubrey was right. The little blue compact was no longer in the space where it had been left. "That means she or someone must have come back for it." He turned and looked up at the foundation's roof. "Was that camera repaired?"

"I hope so," said Aubrey.

They both hurried back inside.

It took only a moment for Mary to access the tapes from the previous evening and send them to Aubrey's computer in her office. She fast-forwarded to the point at which the foundation was closed. Emily's car was the only one in the lot. Again, she fast-forwarded until a red sports car pulled into the lot.

Emily got out of the passenger side and ran over to her own car.

Isaac stood peering over her shoulder at the screen. "Do you recognize that car?"

"It looks like Duncan's 'fun' car. Not the one he drives to work every day. He has pictures of it in his office where most people put pictures of their kids or pets and people they love."

"I'd say we need to get a warrant to search Duncan's place or at least go over there," said Isaac.

"Getting a warrant will take time, won't it?"

"Yes," said Isaac.

Aubrey sat back in her chair. She rewound the tape. "You're the expert. What would you say Emily's body language communicates?" She pushed the play button.

Isaac watched Emily get out of the car and run over to her own. Right before she opened the door, she looked side to side. "Do you see the way she glances around? I'd say she's nervous, maybe even afraid."

"Like she's expecting someone to come at her?"

"Yes, that could be it or just in a general heightened state of fear." Isaac leaned closer to the screen. "Play it one more time."

Aubrey pushed some buttons and rewound. "I don't know how to slow it down, but I can stop it if needed."

He watched again. "She gets out of Duncan's car of her own free will. She's not pushed. He doesn't get out and watch her. There is no indication she is being held against her will."

"But we don't know for sure if it is even Duncan in the car. We don't see him."

"Right, it's a reasonable assumption that because it's

his car, he's the one driving, but that isn't visible on the tape," said Isaac.

The action ended with the red car pulling out of the lot and Emily's blue car following. And then they were staring at an empty lot.

Isaac straightened his spine. He hesitated in sharing the next piece of information. "Given that she is in a separate car, if she wanted to get away from Duncan, she could just drive away from him at this point."

"Are you saying that if Duncan is up to something, Emily is a willing accomplice?"

"I'm just saying that the tape doesn't show signs of coercive behavior on Duncan's part...if it is him in the car. They seem to be working together." Isaac put a supportive hand on Aubrey's shoulder. "These are just theories. Nothing is conclusive yet. The tape is only one piece of evidence."

Aubrey shook her head. "What has my sister gotten herself involved in?" She turned to face him. "We have to go over to Duncan's house. I'm his coworker. I can knock on his door. We can see if Emily is there. We won't have to wait for a warrant."

"If Duncan is up to something," said Isaac, "that might be dangerous."

"Isaac, please. I feel like time is running out. We have to find her. You and Freddy will be with me," she said.

"I want to know where she is as bad as you do." He shook his head. "We don't know what we're dealing with here." Really, there was no one else who could go. Ruby and Brandie were occupied dealing with other parts of the case, and Tanner hadn't shown up yet.

"If Emily is there, I think it should be me to try to talk to her. If she just knows that no matter what she's done, I want her in my life and I love her, maybe she'll feel safe telling me what's going on."

"I suppose it's worth a shot." They left Aubrey's office, walked out of the building and got in the K-9 vehicle. Aubrey recited Duncan's home address, which was about a ten-minute drive from the foundation.

Isaac drove through a neighborhood of immaculate houses with large groomed yards. He stopped on the street by the house number Aubrey had given him. No cars were parked in the driveway.

"He probably keeps that sports car garaged," Aubrey said as she studied the area.

"Any of the vehicles on the street look like his other car?"

Aubrey studied the parked cars and then shook her head. "Emily's car isn't here either."

The street looked virtually abandoned at this hour, no one out walking a dog or pushing a baby carriage. Probably all working professionals.

They got out and tried the doorbell. Isaac indicated that Aubrey needed to stand to one side, so his body provided some cover for her in case they were dealing with a man who had killed before. When he glanced through the large front window, there didn't appear to be any activity inside. No lights had been left on.

Aubrey pressed the doorbell again.

He tugged on her sleeve, indicating they should go back to his car. "Let's watch the street for a bit. See if anyone shows up."

They got back in the SUV.

Isaac's phone buzzed. It was Officer Lansbury.

"We got a match from the interior of that storage room. Nathan Wharton was in there at some point. There is no way to tell what he took. A spot on the shelf close to the fingerprint isn't covered in dust, so something was probably sitting there."

"Interesting," said Isaac. "And then Nathan later died suspiciously after he thought he was going to come into some money."

"We'll let you know if there are any more developments," said Officer Lansbury.

"Just so you know. Right now, Duncan LaRoy is a person of interest. We got video evidence that he aided Emily Smith in coming back to the foundation to get her car."

"I remember meeting the guy the day we got the call about the break-in," said Lansbury. "We'll keep a look out for him."

"Keep me posted," said Isaac.

He and Aubrey sat in the vehicle together watching the street. "How long has Duncan worked at that foundation?"

"Years. I think he came there as a PhD candidate. I heard rumors that he didn't like it when Leandra was hired as the director," said Aubrey. "He thought the job should be his."

"My theory is that Nathan Wharton, who probably knew how to bypass that key card to get into the storage room given his skill set, was hired to go in and get something of value, maybe the research Christopher talked about."

"If Duncan had signed out for the key card, that would have made him look guilty," said Aubrey.

Isaac nodded. "Nathan thought he'd get a cut of the deal but instead he ends up dead. That thumb drive had to have been made in advance of the crime, so whoever is behind this wanted a record of everyone involved that might be able to point the finger at him," said Isaac.

"If Duncan is the one behind this, he must still need

Emily alive for whatever reason." Aubrey rubbed her temples, a sign that she was frustrated. "Or Emily is a coconspirator and doesn't realize she could end up dead."

"It scary to think about what that research could be used for. Dimitri was probably after it to weaponize it."

"Russia is second only to the United States for the number of volcanoes they have," Aubrey said.

They sat watching the street for another twenty minutes before Isaac pulled out and rolled down the street. They passed a park.

"Wait," said Aubrey. "Stop the car."

Isaac found a parking space on the street bordering the edge of the park.

Before he could stop her, Aubrey burst out of the SUV and ran back toward a parking lot by the park.

Not taking the time to unload Freddy, Isaac raced after her.

She stopped by a car that was half on the pavement and half on the grass. "This is Emily's car."

"Are you sure?"

She peered in the passenger-side window. "That's the wooden cross I gave her that is hanging from the rearview mirror."

Isaac walked around to the other side of the car. The driver's-side door was slightly ajar as if she had been pulled from the vehicle or had been in such a hurry that she hadn't had time to close it.

Aubrey had come around to where he was.

He surveyed the park, not seeing anything that drew his attention or anyone who looked like Emily. When he touched the hood, it was cold. The car had been here for a while.

He glanced back in Aubrey's direction.

"Isaac, what if my sister is already dead?"

FIFTEEN

While Isaac coordinated with the local police after calling about Emily's abandoned car, Aubrey sat in the SUV and fought off the dark thoughts that kept rising to the surface about her sister. Emily was a willing accomplice in something sinister. Emily had been forced against her will to do something wrong. Emily was no longer alive. She remembered the last time she'd seen her sister, that day at the foundation. The look of shame on her sister's face was etched into Aubrey's brain. She'd seen that look before when they were younger and Emily had gotten into trouble for missing school or shoplifting.

From the back seat where he sat in his kennel, Freddy whimpered.

Aubrey turned to face the beagle. She reached in and petted his head. "You understand how scary this all is, don't you?"

After looking at his phone, Isaac walked back toward the K-9 vehicle and got in. "The local police will take the car in and have a forensic guy look it over."

"What would they even be looking for?"

Isaac put his hands on the steering wheel and let out a breath. "Signs of foul play. Minute blood spatter. We can't rule anything out."

Aubrey ran her fingers through her hair trying to quell

the rising fears. It wasn't just Emily who was on her mind either. What Christopher had said in the research room, that experiments had been done to make volcanoes explode on purpose, meant that what had been taken could have horrifying consequences.

She stared through the windshield. The way the car was situated, it appeared that Emily had been going so fast that she rolled over the curb onto the grass. Was she being chased?

"I heard back from Ruby. She did track down the restaurant where Michael had lunch with the Russian and the other man," said Isaac.

"Did any of the employees remember what the other man looked like?"

Isaac shook his head. "Kind of vague. A tall older man in good shape, brown hair."

"That describes Duncan."

"And a ton of other guys," said Isaac.

"I say we go back to the foundation. Maybe we can get permission to unlock Duncan's office or maybe he said something to Christopher that might tell us what is going on with him. I can't just wait in that motel room."

Isaac nodded. "Let's get that done."

She wondered if he felt like the clock was ticking for Emily like she did.

He turned onto the road that led to the foundation.

Her mind whirled with all the pieces of information. "It's like a riddle, isn't it?"

"What do you mean?"

"What do a rock climber, a computer hacker, a Russian and a banker have in common?" Aubrey stared out the front window as despair overtook her. "Other than they are all dead now."

"Here are the puzzle pieces that we have so far. We

know Michael was killed because he could identify the man who was trying to do the deal with the Russian." Isaac took a tight curve on the winding road. "Michael was panicked when he saw the dead Russian in the newspaper, so maybe he already saw red flags in dealing with the man behind this."

He drove past the public part of the foundation. This late in the day, there were fewer tourists. He circled around to the employee parking lot, where there were still a few cars. They got out of the vehicle. Isaac's attention was drawn to the trees surrounding the lot. He placed a protective arm across Aubrey's back. "Let's get inside."

Aubrey had the sense that something bad was going to happen seconds before the explosion of the first rifle shot hammered her eardrums.

Isaac shielded her with his body as they both fell on the asphalt of the parking lot. The shot had come from the same place as before—the surrounding trees. Her heart pounded.

They crawled toward the front bumper, which provided cover and faced the doors of the building.

"Stay low and get inside. I'm going after this guy," said Isaac.

She angled her head around the bumper, staring at the trees and not seeing any sign of the person who had just taken a shot at them. "Are you sure that's a good idea?"

"He can't shoot us both at the same time. I can release Freddy from his kennel remotely. He and I will go get this guy. While all the attention is on me, you run inside where it's safe."

Isaac could die walking into the trees where there was an armed man. She kissed him quickly. "Be careful."

He locked her into his blue-eyed gaze momentarily, nodded and then slipped to the side of the vehicle where he would be exposed. She ran to the entrance and reached for the door.

Another shot reverberated behind her.

Once inside, she stepped away from the glass doors. She could see Isaac and Freddy as they headed across the lot, moving from car to car, and then they disappeared into the trees.

Her breath caught in her throat as she watched.

No one was in the reception area. Mary had already left for the day. A few cars were still in the lot, so someone was around.

A male intern wandered through the lobby area holding some sample containers.

Still trying to recover from the attack, Aubrey stepped toward him. "Is Christopher still here?"

"Yes, he asked me to grab these for him." The intern held up the containers and took a step closer to her. "Are you okay? You seem upset."

She didn't want to explain what had happened. "I just need to know where Christopher is."

"He's in the new simulation lab."

"Have you seen Duncan at all today?"

The intern turned in a half circle. "You know, I thought he was in his office briefly just a little bit ago."

Her heart leaped. Duncan had been here. She glanced toward his office, where the door, which had been previously locked, was now open. "You didn't talk to him?"

The intern shook his head. "My job is to be Christopher's assistant."

"Can you tell Christopher I'd like to talk to him when he has a moment?"

"Sure, I can do that." The intern disappeared down a hallway.

When she peered outside the window again, the park

police car was headed toward the lot. Isaac must have called for backup.

Both officers headed toward the trees. Officer Nielson remained in view while Lansbury ran into the forest. Aubrey didn't hear any more shots.

A long tense moment passed. First, Officer Lansbury emerged and stepped back into the parking lot. He looked winded and distressed and he was talking on his radio.

Where was Isaac?

Nielson and Lansbury got into their vehicle and pulled out of the lot just as she spotted Isaac and Freddy coming out at a different spot a ways up the road.

Isaac stepped toward the building's doors. She felt a rush of gratitude when she saw he was safe. She ran to meet him and opened the door. She threw her arms around him but did not hug him long. "I'm glad you're okay."

"We couldn't find him," said Isaac. "I think the guy took two shots and ran."

"Maybe he got into a car and drove away like before?"

"I don't know. We didn't hear the sound of a car starting up. Nielson and Lansbury went to see if they could find where he might have parked a vehicle. There's no obvious place to hide a car close by."

Fear invaded her psyche. "The shooter is still out there?"

He must have picked up on her trepidation. He cupped her chin in his fingers. "Hey, it's okay. I'm here."

Afraid that something bad might happen to him, she had kissed Isaac impulsively in the parking lot. But now as she looked into his eyes, she did not regret it. Here was a man who was willing to risk his own life to protect her.

She could feel the spark of electricity between them as he smiled faintly and kissed her forehead. But then he stepped back from her. He chose to move out of the force field of attraction, making it clear the moment had been temporary. He glanced around the empty lobby. "This place is getting ready to close down."

"Christopher and an intern are the only ones left still working, but Duncan was here earlier. I think it would be best to wait to talk to Christopher once he is out of the lab. He gets really cranky when you interrupt him. Maybe Duncan said something to him."

Aubrey hurried toward Duncan's office praying she would get some answers about what was going on. When she opened the door, Duncan's computer was turned off. Several maps were laid out on his desk.

Aubrey glanced at them. The maps were from years ago of different parts of the volcano. "Not sure why he pulled these out. There is much more updated and inter-active stuff on the computer. Way more accurate, and you can make them 3D and everything."

"For some reason, he wanted to look at the older stuff."

"Yes, for some reason." She filed through the maps again. The legend in the corner said they had all been done by the same man, Richard Fowler. They were for both interior and exterior parts of Mount St. Helens. "He was looking for an exact location."

"We know Duncan came back here and left. His car is not in the lot. Though he could park elsewhere if he didn't want to be tracked down."

She stared at the maps for a long moment.

"Why don't we go back down to that research room and see if we can figure out what was taken? Maybe there was some kind of record or filing system."

"We can't get into the room. Not only do you have to sign for the key card, Leandra's the only one who can authorize it and hand the key card over. She's gone for the day," said Aubrey.

"These maps must not have been in the locked research room."

"They are so old," said Aubrey. "They might have been in the other storage room. I just wonder what Duncan is up to. Why is he being so evasive?" It could have been Duncan who shot at her from the trees.

She was already moving toward Mary's counter where the record of sign-outs would be. Aubrey first pulled the clipboard for people signing out to do field research. Duncan hadn't signed out to do any today and yet he had been absent from the office most of the day.

Isaac followed her. "Yet he risked being seen to look at those maps. Something must be urgent. What's on those maps?"

"Different interior and exterior parts of the volcano. There's no special marking on any of them." In the short time her sister had worked at the foundation, it seemed to Aubrey the person Emily had interacted with the most at work was Duncan. Something was going on between them.

Her chest felt tight, and all her muscles tensed. "What do we do now, Isaac?"

Isaac shook his head. "Tanner texted me that he was delayed, so he should be here anytime now. I can check in with Brandie and Ruby. I don't want to do anything without backup."

Officers Nielson and Lansbury must not have tracked down the shooter from the woods or his car, or they would have notified him.

Aubrey stepped across the carpet. "Are you hungry? I think I have some crackers and fruit in my office."

He followed her. "I could use a bite of something."

She rifled through a lower drawer and offered him a banana. "That will hold you until we get something more substantial."

Her green-eyed gaze rested on him for a long moment.

Was he reading too much into the way she looked at him, seeing affection or admiration that was just in his head? Just his wishful thinking? He wasn't imagining the kiss she'd given him earlier, before he'd headed into the woods after the shooter. He clenched his jaw. Maybe it was okay to entertain such thoughts, but his mind always returned to the realization that she could be setting him up to hurt him again.

The connection he felt to her now made him wonder if there was more to the story of why she had broken up with him in such a cruel way. Such action ran counter to the kind woman he had gotten reacquainted with. It didn't even fit who she was ten years ago…or who he thought she was anyway.

She offered him one of the chairs.

He wiped his mind clean of the confusion raging in his head about Aubrey. He needed to keep his focus on the case.

A text from Ruby told him that they had had no further developments. He called Brandie and suggested if she wasn't too tired, she could stake out Duncan's house. Emily had probably been staying there judging from how close her car had been found to the place. Why she had fled was unknown.

The intern poked his head in the office door. "There you are. Took me a minute to find you."

Aubrey looked up. "Did something happen?"

"Yes. I saw Duncan leaving the equipment checkout room just a minute ago," said the intern. "I tried to stop him to let him know you were looking for him, but he ignored me and ran for the door. The guy was in a big hurry."

Isaac rose to his feet. Duncan was clearly up to something.

SIXTEEN

Aubrey jumped up and ran over to the intern. "Did you see which way Duncan went?"

"He had a car parked by the door outside. That's why I couldn't catch him." The intern pointed toward the road that lead to the viewing areas and the trailhead. "He drove that way."

It appeared that Duncan was headed toward the trail where Aubrey had been shot at.

"Did you see what he got out of the equipment room?" She stepped out into the main area of the floor and hurried to glance out at the parking lot. No sign of Duncan's car.

The intern followed her. "Whatever it was, he'd already stuffed it in his backpack when I saw him."

After thanking the intern, Aubrey rushed toward the equipment room. "We have to figure out what he took. If he took poles, he's headed to the top. Otherwise he's on the easy trail."

She raced inside the equipment room. A set of poles was missing. There was an empty hook where climbing gear was hung. "Climbing gear?" Where was Duncan planning on going? Inside the volcano?

Her mind was racing as she grabbed the contracted poles and tossed them toward Isaac. A picture was starting to come together in her head. "Hans Hilstead was a climber. What if Duncan hid something up there with Hans's help, and he dropped the thumb drive by accident? And now he's gone up there to get back what he hid."

"So he hired Nathan to take something valuable out of the research room and hid it in a place no one would look, somewhere in the volcano," said Isaac.

"Only I had just put in to do research in that area." Aubrey hurried back into Duncan's office where the maps were still laid out. She stared at the one that would be closest to where she had been shot at. Nothing was marked or circled on the map.

Isaac had followed her. "There is one thing I don't understand. If he needed Hans's help the first time, how would he climb alone this time?"

"I'm not sure. We won't know anything until we catch up with Duncan," said Aubrey. "Maybe he isn't by himself. Maybe Emily is helping him." She didn't want to entertain that thought for long. She wanted to think the best of her sister.

She wondered too why Duncan had the maps out if he knew where the hiding place was. Maybe he had just sent Hans up there by himself. All she knew was that they needed to catch up with Duncan.

She ran to her office and grabbed her backpack and then another from the equipment room. "He's got at least a twenty-minute head start on us."

She pulled the climbing gear off the hook.

"Wait a second, Aubrey. We could be facing a man who has already killed people. I can't put you in that kind of vulnerable position."

"If climbing is going to be involved, it will probably take two people. You know I am a good climber."

She heard a deep unfamiliar voice behind Isaac. "I heard you two might need a little help."

Isaac stepped to one side, so Aubrey had a view of a tall man with sandy-brown hair. A sleek-looking boxer dog stood beside him.

"Aubrey, this is Tanner Ford and his partner, Britta. He's with the PNK9 unit as well."

"Looks like I'm just in time," said Tanner.

"How did you get in?"

Tanner held up a key card. "It was on the ledge by the door."

Aubrey had been in such a hurry, she'd set her key card down and forgot to pick it up. Such an unsafe thing to do.

Tanner pointed to the climbing gear. "Looks like we're going on a bit of an adventure."

"Do you know how to climb with gear, Tanner?" Aubrey held up the ropes.

Tanner shook his head.

"It's settled then. I'll go up with you two. Tanner and his dog will be the extra protection we need." She gave Isaac a look that indicated she wasn't going to back down.

Isaac shook his head. He reached out to Tanner and cupped his shoulder. "You and Britta are just in time, my friend."

"Other than the inside of the volcano, I don't know where Duncan would be going that he needs climbing gear," said Aubrey.

"Maybe Duncan didn't know either." Isaac pointed toward the maps in Duncan's office. "Maybe he's making an educated guess. There are some unanswered questions."

"I feel like I lost the plot here," said Tanner.

"I'll get you up to speed. It's a long hike up there," said Isaac. "We've got to hurry."

Knowing that it would be dark by the time they got to the top of the volcano, Aubrey grabbed headlamps as well.

Tanner and Britta followed in their K-9 car while Isaac made his way up the road past the viewing areas.

Aubrey could not put the puzzle pieces together as to what was going on. She pulled out her phone. "I need to talk to Christopher before we lose cell reception. He's been here longer than me."

She dialed Christopher's number. He picked up after the third ring. "Christopher, it's Aubrey. Do you know who Richard Fowler is? He might connect to the break-in and the attacks on me."

"Not offhand. The name sounds somewhat familiar."

"He would have worked at the foundation or done some mapping for it."

"He's not anyone I ever worked with. Duncan would know. He's been there longer than even Leandra."

"I don't suppose Duncan ever talked about hiding places on the volcano."

"Hiding places? What's this about, Aubrey?"

"I'll explain later. I need you to do something for me. Maybe there are old employment records in the storage room that's open, or something that might tell us who Richard Fowler was and why those maps on Duncan's desk are important."

"You were in Duncan's office." A note of suspicion entered Christopher's voice.

"Please, Christopher. My sister's life may depend on us getting answers."

"Okay, I'll help you," said Christopher. "I was just wrapping up my report on some tests I ran today."

"I'm headed up to the site where I was attacked. Two police officers are with me. Once we hit the boulder field, cell reception will be sketchy," said Aubrey. "I'll try to contact you before then."

Aubrey, Isaac and Tanner, plus their K 9 partners, arrived at the trailhead. The only other car parked there was Duncan's everyday car. Now they knew for sure this was where he'd gone. They unloaded the dogs and slipped into their backpacks. Isaac took a quick look at Duncan's vehicle but found it locked. He leaned close to the window to peer inside. Then turned to the other two and shook his head. "Nothing significant in there."

Once they were beneath the tree canopy that surrounded the trail, it was much harder to see even though sunset was still a couple of hours away. They walked at a steady pace, with Tanner and Britta taking the lead.

The trail widened out, and Aubrey and Isaac were able to walk side by side with Freddy between them.

The sense of urgency and the fact that they might be facing a showdown with a man who had killed four people already made Aubrey think that time was short. What if one of them died? Isaac would never know the real reason why she'd broken up with him. She cared deeply about him. Not the eighteen-year-old Isaac still under his parents' influence, but the man he'd become. Maybe she even loved him.

This might be her last chance to let him know what really happened ten years ago. Would he reject her anyway? Was he still too wounded to open his heart to her? He might not even believe his mother was capable of such a controlling move.

She was willing to take that chance just to tell the truth. "Isaac, all those years ago when I broke up with you…"

Isaac stared straight ahead. "That was a long time ago, Aubrey. The past is the past."

His answer was abrupt, seeming to indicate he had no desire to talk about what happened ten years ago. She wasn't going to give up that easily.

"We could be walking into a firestorm here. One of us might not make it." She grabbed his sleeve, forcing him to stop and face her. "I want you to know why. The night after we announced our engagement, your mother came to my room and said that if I went forward with the marriage, I would be robbing you of your potential and future."

Isaac stared at her for a long moment but didn't say anything. It had grown too dark for her to read his expression clearly.

"She said I wasn't the kind of woman who would be an asset to someone like you. I guess I still saw myself as the poor little orphan girl back then. I believed what she told me. I thought I was doing what was best for you."

"Aubrey, I had no idea my mother had done that. All I got was a breakup text." His voice was raw with emotion. "You put my life into a tailspin. It took years to recover."

"That wasn't my intention." Though Isaac kept his voice level, she could feel his ire. Her voice grew softer. "I thought I was helping you."

Isaac stared at her for a long moment before speaking. "You waited all these years to tell me that."

"At that time, I thought your mother was right. That I would just hold you back from the life you deserved. I thought you would meet someone else who would fit in with your family better. I assumed that had happened. I wouldn't have come back and interfered with your marriage."

"Well, I didn't get married to someone else, did I?"

Isaac was still upset. She wasn't sure what she could

say or if she needed to. She had done her part; she'd told him the whole story.

"Hey, guys." Tanner stood at the top of the trail, a silhouette in the dimming light. Britta took up a position next to him. "Come on, double-time. I was told this mission was time sensitive."

The tension from the moment hung in the air with no sense of resolution for Aubrey. She'd taken the risk and let him know why she had so abruptly exited his life. It was up to Isaac to decide what to do about that.

The emotion she heard in his voice conveyed that he had not healed from the old wounds.

Isaac resumed some small talk with Tanner. He spoke to Aubrey only to warn her about a tree root on the trail.

Aubrey's phone rang. "Christopher, what did you find out?"

"Richard Fowler and Duncan were work colleagues before you or I ever came here. There's no work records or anything, but I found a photo of them in a newspaper article in one of the file cabinets in the storage room."

"Good job, Christopher. That took some digging. I wonder if Richard Fowler's primary job was mapping the volcano inside and out."

"I'll let you know if I find anything else out about who he was," said Christopher. "I'll snoop a while longer and then I got to get some dinner."

"Thanks, Christopher. I'm about to go out of cell range once we hit the boulder field. Text me anything you find."

She pressed the disconnect button.

The trail narrowed, forcing them to walk single file. Tanner and Britta stayed in front, and Isaac let Aubrey get in front of him so she would be in the middle, which probably provided her with a degree of protection.

There was no telling what kind of danger lay ahead.

They didn't know if Duncan was at the top of the volcano or waiting along the trail somewhere, ready to ambush them if he saw he'd been followed.

Isaac tried to keep his mind on the task ahead of them, uncertain of what they faced. What Aubrey had told him, the reason behind the breakup, wrecked him all over again. It didn't surprise him about what his mother had done. Though he knew his mother had loved him and only wanted the best for him, Susan McDane had always been fixated on a life that reflected wealth and success and wanted the same for her sons.

What bothered him was that Aubrey had not fought for their relationship or at least told him why they couldn't be together. He had never thought of her as somehow less than because of her background. From the moment he'd met her, her sense of adventure and the clarity she had about what she wanted to do with her life had energized him.

It was only when he joined law enforcement that he realized that the profession where he felt most at home was different from what his parents had envisioned for him. They had not been happy with his choice but came to accept it before their untimely deaths.

His steps held an intensity that matched his thoughts. The trees thinned as they encountered more lava rocks.

A noise that sounded like a breaking branch caused Isaac to spin around while his hand hovered over his gun. His heartbeat drummed in his ears as he stared at the trees below.

"Did you hear that?"

"Yes," said Tanner. Britta licked her muzzle and let out a tiny whine.

Aubrey turned as well and peered over his shoulder.

"There's lots of wildlife and nocturnal critters out at this hour."

He waited a moment longer, satisfied that the noise was just something that belonged in the forest.

As the boulder field overtook the trees, the hike became more strenuous. Aubrey took up the lead with her headlamp on to light the way. She forged a path that took them through the least treacherous route. If Duncan was looking over his shoulder, the light would give them away, but traversing the field in the dark would only cause injury.

Britta had the climbing skills of a mountain goat. Though Isaac had brought the carrier for Freddy, it was just as easy to lift his light body over the larger boulders.

When the boulders gave way to the ash beach, they pulled out their poles from the backpacks and lengthened them.

He studied the area up ahead, not seeing anything that would indicate where Duncan had gone. "Let's move toward where Aubrey was attacked. But keep the use of the light to a minimum."

Aubrey switched off her headlamp.

The path led them along the side of the volcano with the crater in the distance. They came to the place where they had found the thumb drive. Isaac had marked it with a flag.

Isaac turned a half circle.

"There. I saw a flash of light up by the peak," Tanner said.

Isaac looked where Tanner had indicated but didn't see anything. "Lead the way," he said.

They increased their pace. The terrain turned rocky again, which was easier to navigate than the pumice beach. Isaac kept glancing toward the peak, hoping to see what Tanner had spotted.

They were moving at an incline with Tanner hiking at an intense pace. The dogs kept up with them.

Tanner stopped, out of breath, and pointed up. "I think I saw the flash of light right about there."

They were still about a hundred feet from the peak. The night had grown dark, and the rock was black. He couldn't see anything. Isaac had no choice but to take out his flashlight. He stepped forward and then glanced over his shoulder. "Aubrey, move in closer to Tanner."

Aubrey obliged. She understood the risk. If Duncan was up there, if he had a gun, they would be in a vulnerable position. Isaac unclipped his holster strap and moved closer to where Tanner had pointed. Something metal caught the light.

He moved up even closer, hoping for the shapes to become more distinct. The metal was a carabiner used for climbing. He could just make out the yellow of a climbing rope that had to be draped down the interior of the crater.

Aubrey and Tanner had both moved closer to him, so they saw what he had shone the light on. "Do you think Duncan is down there?"

"I don't know," said Isaac. "Not sure how steep the interior of the volcano is. I imagine it's pretty precarious. Climbing solo would be a bad idea. Safer to have someone to belay you."

"Let's get as close to the peak as we can," said Tanner. "Britta and I will stand watch."

"Freddy will go with me in the carrier. There were plenty of electronics in that research room. If there is anything like that down there, Freddy will find it."

Isaac removed his duty belt knowing it would be too cumbersome to climb with. He placed the gun in his waistband, then moved to pull his carrier from the back-pack that he'd thrown on the ground.

He laid the carrier down so Freddy could step into it. "Come on, buddy, you know the drill."

Once Freddy was secured, he lifted the carrier and pulled the straps over his shoulders with Aubrey's help. Freddy gave a grunt as he faced forward.

They trekked the remaining distance to the peak, where the other climbing equipment had been abandoned. Isaac held out a protective hand, indicating Aubrey should stay back. He pulled his gun from his waistband and peered over the edge, letting his eye go where the rope dangled. He expected to be shot at or to see Duncan's broken body lying on a ledge. Instead, all he saw was the jagged lava rock. "He's not down here. Not that I can see."

Aubrey moved closer to him. "Maybe we scared him away." She turned, staring out into the darkness.

There were plenty of rocky hiding places. "Maybe he already got what he wanted. He could return to his car and not be seen by us if he stayed off the trail."

"It seems like we would have heard him at the point we crossed paths. Plus, Tanner thought he saw lights up here," said Aubrey.

He shone the light again, seeing several ledges. "I don't know why, but I was expecting a boiling cauldron of fire down there."

"All the activity is taking place beneath the surface of the earth in this part of the volcano. Other parts have steam eruptions and gas escaping. Those parts are closed to the public. Trust me, Mount St. Helens is a busy volcano."

"Belay Freddy and me down. If there is anything electronic down there, Freddy will be a big help. I haven't done this in a while," said Isaac. "I might be a little rusty." He grabbed the flashlight from his duty belt and put it in his jacket pocket.

When they were dating, climbing had been one of their favorite things to do together. Aubrey had taught him how to climb. It was an exercise in trust to have your partner control the rope while you rappelled down a mountain.

Isaac hooked into the climbing harness while Aubrey secured the ropes.

"Ready?"

Their heads were only inches apart. Though it was too dark to see her face, he could smell her floral-scented perfume.

"Ready," he said.

Aubrey let out the line as his feet sought a secure hold. His body was at a forty-five-degree angle as he climbed down for a few feet. "I'm going to try to hit that first ledge."

With springlike action, he pushed off the wall of the mountain. The rope made a zinging noise, and he sailed down. He turned his head to get a bead on where the ledge was. He could feel the warmth of Freddy's body as the dog remained still.

His feet found the ledge, which was maybe three feet at its narrowest. He stepped toward a wider part. The harness would keep Isaac from falling, but a leash would be the only thing securing the dog once he was not in his carrier.

Isaac took a deep breath and moved to release Freddy from the carrier. "Okay, partner, let's see what we can find."

SEVENTEEN

Isaac lifted the carrier off his shoulders and laid it on the ledge. After unzipping the back, he let Freddy step free of the leg holes. He snapped the leash on the beagle and gave the command to search. The dog put his nose to the ground. The ledge was at least ten feet long. If Freddy did fall on the narrower part of it, Isaac might be able to save him by pulling him up with the leash. Still, the situation was precarious.

Freddy moved along the ledge with a deft agility. Once he reached the end, he turned around and stopped at a spot he had previously hesitated at but not alerted on.

The dog put his front paws on the wall of the volcano and sniffed. He sat down.

"What's going on?" Aubrey called from above.

"Freddy alerted on something."

Isaac pulled his flashlight out. He saw several small crevices. He felt inside the holes, thinking there might be another thumb drive in them, but he found nothing. There had to be something here. It would be rare for Freddy to have a false alert in an environment where electronics were not abundant.

His hand felt along the wall of the mountain until he found a loose rock. He could move the rock when he pushed on it, but it was wedged so tightly, he couldn't get a fingerhold to pull it out.

Freddy sat at attention while Isaac pulled his pocket-knife out, aimed his flashlight and stuck the knife in the crevice. He was able to pull the rock forward far enough to get a fingerhold and yank it out. The rock clattered onto the ledge.

Isaac put his hand in the hole and felt around. At first his hands grazed over the rough texture of the rock, but then his fingertips felt something colder and smoother. Metal perhaps.

He pressed his arm as deeply into the hole as he could so that the rock dug into his armpit. Whoever had hidden the item here may have brought a tool to push it deep into the mountain and another to pull it out. He felt a corner. There was a metal box hidden in the tunnellike crevice.

Isaac glanced down at Freddy's expectant face. "Good job, boy." He retrieved one of the treats he always carried with him and placed his open palm under Freddy's nose so he could have it. Tossing the treat meant that Freddy might end up falling.

Isaac tilted his head. He could barely make out Aubrey's face as she stared down at him. "I need something to function as a hook. Like a tree branch."

"I'll see what I can find," she said.

She disappeared from view. He could hear her shouting at Tanner. Aubrey was smart not to abandon the ropes that kept him from free-falling. A moment later, her head reappeared. "Tanner is looking for something that might work. There is not a lot of vegetation this high up."

Isaac pulled his arm out of the hole knowing it was pointless to try to get it out with just his hand. The hole was not big enough to put both arms in to try to work the box loose.

Aubrey reappeared a moment later. "This is the best we can do on such short notice. I am weaving it through one of the carabiners Duncan left behind and sending it down."

He could hear her moving around, her feet scraping the ground, and then he saw the glint of metal with something long and narrow sticking out of both sides.

As the rope came closer to him, he realized it was the flag on a metal rod that he had used to mark where the thumb drive had been found. Perfect.

He lifted his arm to grab it, praying that it wouldn't fall out of the carabiner before he had it in his hands. Once he held the metal rod, he pulled it out of the carabiner and bent the end that didn't have the flag on it to create a hook. He moved quickly to stick the rod into the hole and place it in the handle on the box. The metal box scraped against rock as he slid it closer to the opening. Finally, he was able to pull it out. It was a simple metal box with no lock, just a fastener that held it shut.

"What did you find?" Aubrey called to him from above.

He flipped it open. The box contained CDs and floppy disks as well as some paper materials underneath the electronics. It was too dark to read the labels on the disks and CDs. This was worth killing for? He shone the flashlight on it. The label on the top had a date and reference numbers to a simulation. He could look at it more closely later.

Isaac tilted his head. "I'm sending it up to you on the carabiner, and then you need to get Freddy and I back up this rock wall." After clicking the box shut, Isaac hooked the handle through the carabiner.

Aubrey drew it up while he got Freddy back in his carrier. He winced every time the box banged against the wall of the mountain. What if the latch fell open and the contents tumbled hundreds of feet into the abyss of the volcano?

Isaac commanded Freddy to step into his carrier, and then he closed the zipper that ran up the back of it.

He waited for Aubrey to secure the ropes before he attempted to lift the carrier and put his arms through the straps. If he lost his balance, he could fall to his death taking his partner with him.

"The box is safe and sound, and I'm ready to belay you up." The ropes went taut.

He bent and picked up the carrier. Freddy licked Isaac's fingers. Getting back up would be way more strenuous than coming down.

When he found his first foothold in the wall just above the ledge, Aubrey responded by tightening the rope. The leverage of the ropes would give her the strength to hold him in place or to break a fall if he slipped from the wall, but most of the climb depended on Isaac finding secure hand- and footholds on the steep wall.

Freddy remained still. The dog seemed to pick up on the need not to wiggle too much and throw off his partner's balance.

Isaac scaled the wall for several feet with Aubrey responding by slacking when he needed to move sideways or drawing it tighter as he climbed up. When he tilted his head, he could see the night sky. Only a few more feet to go.

He heard a noise that sounded like a gunshot. Britta barked somewhere in the distance.

The line zinged through the carabiner. Isaac fell through the air several feet, stopping with a jolt. His heart pounded as he was left swinging back and forth, unable to get close enough to the wall to regain a foothold. He could not see Aubrey when he looked up.

"Aubrey, what's happening?"

Aubrey grabbed the rope from the position where she'd fallen on her behind at the sound of a gunshot. Adrenaline surged through her body as she held the rope. The fall had caused her to give the line too much slack. Even if she turned to look, she doubted she could see what was going on behind her in the dark. She only hoped whoever had fired the shot was not coming for her next and that Tanner was okay. She could not leave Isaac and Freddy stranded.

Quelling the rising panic, she held the line tight and scooted to where she could see Isaac. "Gunshots. Not sure what's happening. We have to hurry." She adjusted the ropes so Isaac could move closer to the wall.

He found a foothold and climbed quickly. She was grateful when his head rose above the rim of the mountain. She reached out to help him climb over.

He hadn't even gotten to his feet when he pulled his gun from his waistband. "Stay behind me."

She picked up the metal box that might have cost lives. Freddy was still in his carrier as Isaac made his way down the mountain. Without any light, she could barely see where she put her feet, let alone what the result of the gunshot had been. Isaac had maybe opted not to use his flashlight fearing if someone was still out there with a gun, it would make them easy targets.

Isaac came to a sudden stop. She halted behind him, peering over his shoulder. A man was lying on the ground. They both ran toward him.

Aubrey dropped to her knees so she could see the man's face. "Duncan?"

Duncan held his hand over his stomach and groaned in pain.

"I tried to help Emily get out of trouble. She didn't want you to know." Duncan laid his head back down. "I'm so sorry."

"Duncan, where is Emily? What has happened to her?"

"Kidnapped." Duncan opened his mouth as if to say more, but then turned his head and closed his eyes. The news of what had happened to Emily was like a knife to her heart.

Isaac checked Duncan's pulse. "He's still alive. He's out cold, he's not going anywhere. We have to get down to where there is cell service. A chopper can get here a lot faster than if we try to carry him out and risk hurting him more. Plus carrying him will slow us down."

"The trail is so precarious in spots, I'm not sure we could even get him to the bottom," said Aubrey.

Why had Duncan come up here for the box and tried to get down to it without help? He must have seen them coming and hid, knowing that they would find the box. From what he said, it sounded like Duncan wasn't part of the crime but had gotten involved to help Emily. He wasn't the man behind all this. The man who had shot at them was.

Aubrey lifted her head when she heard a distant, faint bark. That had to be Britta.

"We need to get down this mountain. If Tanner has gone in pursuit of the shooter, he'll need my help."

Isaac rose to his feet and slipped out of the carrier. Aubrey helped him put it on the ground. "Hauling Freddy through the ash beach will throw my balance off. Besides, he's more sure-footed than I am."

They both retrieved the collapsed poles from beside

the backpacks where they'd left them when they climbed the remainder of the way to the summit of the mountain.

They traversed the beach as quickly as they dared, sliding and recovering until the beach gave way to the boulders. They had not heard Britta or seen Tanner yet.

As they wove through and over the boulders, Isaac stopped twice to see if he had cell reception, and then he kept going.

They hurried through the darkness taking turns carrying the metal box. When she saw the outline of trees up ahead, she willed herself to move faster. The trees grew more abundant. She searched for where the trail might be.

Several times Isaac tried his radio, but Tanner didn't respond.

Isaac checked his cell phone again. He dialed the emergency number, explaining about Duncan and the need for a chopper and giving the location. He also called Ruby and Brandie for backup.

They continued running down the trail. They both heard the distant sound of a dog barking and rushed through the trees toward the noise.

In the dark and without the security of the flat trail, it felt like they were running blindly guided only by the sound of Britta's barking. They jumped over logs and pushed through thick brush, adjusting their direction every time they heard a bark.

Britta burst through the trees, clearly agitated. Yipping and pacing side to side.

"Where's Tanner, girl?"

The dog led them to a small clearing. Tanner lay on his stomach not moving.

Isaac dove to the ground and turned Tanner over. "He's breathing." He slapped the man's cheeks lightly. "Come on back to me, friend." Britta licked Tanner's forehead.

Aubrey peered over Isaac's shoulder.

Tanner shook his head. He attempted to sit up but laid his head back down and placed a hand on the back of it. "Guy hit me in the head when I jumped him and tried to get his gun from him."

"Where did he go?" Aubrey studied the area around her while she gripped the metal box. The attacker had to have come for what they had found in the volcano. Seeing that they were about to retrieve the box, he must have been waiting for the chance to shoot them and take it. Duncan might even have tried to stop him and that was when he was shot.

"We're walking into an ambush," said Aubrey. "He must be waiting for us somewhere along the trail." Unless the attacker thought he had taken Tanner out for good, he had to know he was outnumbered and outgunned. Would he be bold enough to attack them or did he have something else in mind? Aubrey held up the box. "And he probably wants this."

"We have no choice. We have to get down this mountain. Backup is on their way. Maybe we can catch this guy before he jumps us."

"Let's not take the trail then." Tanner sat up, rubbing his head.

That would slow them down substantially, but maybe it was the best option. "I think I can lead us down a more concealed way without getting too far from the trail."

Isaac held out a hand for Tanner, who still seemed a little wobbly.

"We don't need to play defense. We've got two trained officers with guns. As far as we know, we're dealing with one guy who has one gun," said Isaac. "I say we stay hidden and keep an eye out for him."

Aubrey made a mental note of where the trail was before they'd veered off and jogged downhill. Her muscles tensed in a defensive posture like someone expecting to be punched in the stomach. She was aware that any noise they made might give them away. For most of the way, they had a partial view of the trail. She heard no noise and saw nothing that indicated someone was on the trail or close to it.

Isaac and Freddy fell in beside her, but Tanner lagged behind.

When they came to a part of the forest where the brush and foliage was so overgrown it was impossible to get through, she stepped around it toward where she believed the trail to be, though it did not come into sight. The trail wound around the mountain in a serpentine pattern, so it would be easy to lose a sense of where they really were as they moved through the dark.

If they kept working downhill, they should come to the trailhead.

Isaac grabbed Aubrey's hand. "Hey, stop."

"Did you hear something?"

"No." He looked over his shoulder. "No, I'm waiting for Tanner. He's really going slow. I think he's hurt worse than he's letting on."

They waited until Tanner, led by Britta, came back in sight.

"Don't wait on my account," said Tanner. "We're on a mission here."

They had to be getting closer to the trailhead and still there was no sign of the man who had shot Duncan. Above them, she heard the sound of the helicopter that was going to rescue Duncan. She prayed that he would make it out alive.

When she heard the sound of a car, she knew that they

were close to the trailhead parking lot and that someone had just pulled in.

Both Aubrey and Isaac slowed down as the trees thinned out. She lifted her head, trying to get a view of the parking lot. It would be foolhardy to just step out into the open. The culprit had hired help before. Maybe that car indicated they were dealing with more than one armed man.

And then she heard a voice, the same voice that had spoken to her days ago as she ran for life down this mountain. "I know you're there, and I know you have what I want."

Aubrey looked at Isaac, not sure what to do.

He shook his head.

"I think I have something that you want," said the voice.

She could only see part of the parking lot and not where the man who was speaking was.

A female voice filled with anguish reached her ears. "Aubrey, it's me. I messed up. I tried to make things right, and I made everything worse."

Aubrey felt like she'd been punched in the gut. The voice was Emily's.

"I need you to come out where I can see you, Aubrey," the male voice said. "That policeman friend of yours needs to toss his gun where I can see it, since your other police friend is out of commission."

Aubrey looked over her shoulder, not seeing Tanner. Maybe he had lost consciousness.

An intense, heavy silence invaded the air.

"I will give you until the count of five," said the male voice.

"Aubrey, he has a gun to my head." Emily sputtered out the words.

"One. I need to see that gun, Officer."

Aubrey glanced at Isaac as her heart raced. The man had already killed four people. "If you kill my sister, you have nothing to bargain with."

"Ah, there you are. At last, the lady volcanologist responds. I remember seeing an article about you in the newspaper when you were hired. Your work is nothing compared to mine."

Isaac had begun to move sideways through the trees; he made a motion with his hand that she needed to keep the gunman talking. He must be trying to figure out where the man was so he could line up a shot on him. Freddy padded silently beside Isaac.

"So you used to work for the foundation?"

"Quit trying to distract me. Two. Officer, you need to toss that gun out now or she gets it."

Emily let out a fear-filled scream. Isaac had probably been trained to never give up his weapon, but it looked as if Emily's life depended on it.

Isaac threw his gun toward the parking lot. He had to have a backup plan.

"Very nice," said the voice. "Three."

Aubrey felt as though a weight had been placed on her chest. It was a struggle to get a deep breath. She could no longer see Isaac.

"Four."

A gunshot rent the air. Freddy barked. It sounded like it had come from the parking lot aimed into the trees.

"Isaac?"

She didn't hear a reply.

"Five."

Aubrey rushed toward the edge of the trees. "I'm here. I have your stupid box."

A man about Duncan's age and build held a gun to Emily's head.

"There you are."

She glanced toward the trees wondering if Isaac had been shot.

"Please, let my sister go."

"It's not that easy. I need you to put the box about five feet from me and then back away hands in the air."

It seemed that if Isaac had been shot, Freddy would have made more of a ruckus or at least come out to her to let her know.

"Okay, I'll do what you say."

The kidnapper must have parked his car not far away but hidden with Emily locked in it while he went up the mountain to find Duncan. When Aubrey stepped toward the man who held her sister's life in the balance, her whole body trembled. Emily made soft whimpering sounds. It sounded like she was crying.

Aubrey sat the metal box on the ground.

"Now step away. Five steps backward with your arms in the air."

Aubrey complied. Where was Isaac? Did he have something planned or was he lying on the ground bleeding out? The man who held Emily acted as if he only had to deal with Aubrey.

He pushed Emily forward. "Get the box and bring it back to me."

Emily stumbled and walked toward where the metal box was. She bent over and picked it up while the man went from aiming the gun at Emily and then training it on Aubrey.

Emily returned to the man and opened the box. He glanced inside. "Very nice. Close it."

"I gave you what you want. Now let Emily go." Aubrey thought she saw movement behind the car the culprit must have driven up here.

He grabbed Emily by the hair and pulled her back, putting the gun to her head. "Sorry, she's my insurance policy that I get out of here."

"No." Aubrey stepped toward the man.

A shadow came from behind the car. At the same time, Tanner stepped out of the trees, gun drawn with Britta at his side. She realized that the shadow was Isaac.

Shots were fired. Tanner fell to the ground. Another shot exploded around her. The bullet had come close to hitting her. She crawled for the cover of the trees.

Aubrey heard the sounds of wrestling and fists striking flesh.

Another shot filled the air.

She crouched in the tree line, paralyzed with fear as the silence enveloped her. She squeezed her eyes shut and prayed that Isaac and Tanner and Emily were okay.

When she opened them, Freddy was inches from her face. He nudged her with his nose.

Her throat was raw as she tried to speak. "Hey, buddy. What happened?"

He wagged his tail.

"Aubrey?"

Isaac hovered above her. "You can come out. We've got him in custody." He reached out a hand to help her up. He wrapped a supportive arm around her and led her back into the parking lot.

Brandie and Ruby had each come in separate cars. Tanner was leading a handcuffed man toward his vehicle. She didn't see her sister anywhere.

"Where's Emily?"

Her sister stepped out from behind a car and ran toward Aubrey. They embraced.

"I was afraid something bad had happened to you." Tears flowed down Aubrey's face. "I'm so glad you're okay."

"I messed up. I fell for the wrong guy again. Nathan Wharton acted like he was interested in me. He pretended like he wanted to learn all about the place I worked so he could get an idea of the layout. I think he might even have taken my key card for the outside door and replicated it somehow. I am a fool."

She hugged her sister again. "No, don't say that. You're nothing of the sort. You are my sister and I love you."

Isaac stood off to the side. "How does Duncan fit into this?"

"The day the break-in was discovered I figured out what Nathan Wharton had done. I tried to make it right. I didn't want you to find out because I was so ashamed that I messed up again. Anyway, Duncan was always kind to me. When I told him about what had happened, how Nathan wanted to see the basement, he knew exactly who was behind the break-in."

"Let me guess. His name is Richard Fowler."

"Yes. Duncan worked with him years ago. He was unstable. They did not renew his grant, and it was clear he felt slighted and would find a way to get revenge."

They both looked to where Tanner had loaded Richard Fowler into his K-9 vehicle.

"That research could have done some serious damage in the world," said Aubrey.

"Duncan said they closed down the research on ethical grounds," said Emily. "Richard kidnapped me when I was leaving Duncan's house."

"He must have thought he could use you as leverage to get Duncan to go up and get the research," said Isaac. "He was probably planning on killing him and taking the metal box so he could sell the research to the highest bidder."

"Richard just didn't count on us being there," said Aubrey.

"Why didn't you go to the police?"

"Duncan was afraid that Richard would find a way to not get caught," said Emily. "He said Richard was a man with no conscience, but that he could be charismatic and convincing in his lies. Duncan thought he might be able to talk his way out of an arrest."

Anyone who would sell research that could cause the death of people and the destruction of property was evil.

Ruby approached the three of them. "Looks like you have it all under control. Tanner will make sure that guy is booked and put in a cell." Ruby turned to face Emily. "You must be Aubrey's sister. She was really worried about you."

Aubrey wrapped an arm around Emily. "I'm just glad she's okay."

"Why don't we regroup back at the motel? Aubrey has her stuff there anyway." Isaac turned to look at her. "I can give you and your sister a ride to your condo. I'm sure the two of you have some catching up to do."

The realization that she no longer needed to be afraid and looking over her shoulder sunk in. She had put the request in to do the research in the area where the box had been stowed probably around the same time Richard had helped Hans hide it. Her being in that area meant that she might catch him up there or notice something suspicious. Richard had wanted to keep her from snooping around and had been willing to kill her to do that.

Not only did he initially go after her for the thumb drive, but he probably feared she might find the box if she continued her research in that area.

Aubrey realized she could go back to work tomorrow. She could have her old life back. She glanced at Isaac. He locked eyes with her but said nothing. Did she want her old life back? Isaac had been noncommittal when she had shared about why she had broken up with him. *She* had risked rejection by sharing.

"Come on, let's head back to the motel so you can get your stuff." Isaac brushed her arm lightly.

His touch still had the power to make her feet melt in her shoes. Attraction, though, was not the basis to build a relationship. It was only the start. And maybe that had been their mistake years ago. They were both too young to weather a storm of his mother's idea about how his life should look.

Now that they were both older, could they have something deeper together? Did Isaac even want that?

After they stopped at the motel for Aubrey to pick up her stuff, Isaac drove the two women to Aubrey's condo.

He said goodbye to both of them and gave each a hug.

Aubrey knelt on the ground and petted Freddy. "You be good, now. Take care of your partner."

"We'll be in touch with both of you. We have to put together a report, and we will have to take your statements," said Isaac. "The four of us are probably going to spend the night putting together the details of the case so we can do a write-up."

At least Isaac was indicating she would see him again, in an official capacity anyway. Why was she still holding out hope that he cared about her on a personal level? Just because she realized she had feelings for him didn't mean it would be reciprocated.

Emily stepped toward Isaac. "If you find out how Duncan is doing, can you let me know? He helped me a lot."

"Sure, as soon as we get any word," said Isaac. "You ladies have a good night."

She stood on the sidewalk watching the red taillights of his SUV until he turned the corner and was gone.

So that was that; Isaac was going back to his team. His focus was his job, his K-9 partner and his coworkers. She needed to let go of the idea that there would be any resolution to what had happened so many years ago.

"He seemed nice," said Emily.

Emily had not met Isaac when she was engaged to him. That was maybe a story to share for another time.

"Yes, he's one of the good guys," said Aubrey.

As they headed toward her condo, she realized it would probably still be a mess from the break-in. The physical work would be a distraction from thinking about Isaac.

Aubrey gave Emily a sideways hug. "I'm just glad I got my sister back."

"Remember what Dad used to say." Emily followed her sister up the sidewalk.

"What was that?"

"Family is family," said Emily.

Aubrey laughed. "I wonder what he meant by that." She stuck her key in the door and opened it.

"I think he just meant that family is important."

They stepped inside and Aubrey closed the door behind her, seeing the mess. She felt like her heart might break over Isaac.

EIGHTEEN

After a restless night without much sleep, Isaac woke in the motel room. When he peered out the window, Brandie's and Tanner's vehicles were already gone. Isaac and Ruby had agreed to stay behind to do the follow-up interviews with Emily and Aubrey. They'd gotten word that Duncan had pulled through at the hospital but would probably not be ready to make a statement for several days. Isaac had texted Emily that Duncan was going to be okay.

Ruby saw Isaac through the window and waved.

He opened the door.

"There's a coffee hut like two blocks up and one over. Brandie texted me about it. You want to grab a cup with me?"

"Sure," said Isaac.

The sun bathed his skin with warmth as they walked to the coffee hut with their dogs and put in their order.

Once they had their coffee, Ruby took a sip of her drink.

Isaac glanced down at Freddy, who had found a shady spot under a table.

They both took several sips of their coffee. Enjoying the companionable silence that happens between friends. He didn't want to bombard her with questions about Eli

Ballard, but this was the first chance he'd had to talk to her about the situation.

"You okay about Eli turning out to be a suspect?" he asked. "I mean, I know you're not. But you're such a pro that you've hidden your feelings well."

Ruby bit her lip. "I feel awful about it. How could I not have suspected him? How was he able to fool me so easily that he's a good guy? If he's the killer…"

Isaac knew that the chief and other members of the team were working on the Eli Ballard angle and following up on questions. Had he killed Stacey Stark and Jonas Digby in Mount Rainier National Park and then framed Mara for the double homicide? Had he threatened Mara and Asher's father to keep Mara from coming forward?

Isaac prayed they'd have answers soon.

"He fooled all of us," Isaac reminded her. "You can't be so hard on yourself."

She gave him something of a thankful nod. "You look kind of tired," she said, clearly wanting to change the subject. "Did you sleep okay?"

"No, not really," said Isaac.

They sat down at the picnic table by the coffee hut. "Really? I always sleep great after a case is wrapped up."

"I know. I usually do too. I just got a lot on my mind." The thoughts and emotions were tumbling through his head at warp speed. The truth was he had peace about the case. What had made him toss and turn all night was thinking about what Aubrey had told him as to why she had exited his life so abruptly ten years ago. It made sense, but it didn't make the pain of her rejection hurt any less.

Ruby combed her fingers through her dark hair. "I thought I would get Emily's statement and you can get Aubrey's. Does that work for you?"

"Sure." He would see Aubrey one more time. He could simply play the role of police officer or he could respond to what she'd told him. Maybe talking through things meant they might date, but where would that lead? What if they did become close? What he feared the most was opening his heart and being rejected by her all over again. After ten years, he really hadn't recovered. He certainly hadn't ever been willing to give his heart away to any other woman. Maybe that fear had been driving his self-imposed isolation all along. Or maybe he hadn't dated because Aubrey really had been the one for him. The fear of rejection had overshadowed that reality, but now he knew that was true.

Ruby attempted to get his attention by ducking her head so he would look at her. "Penny for your thoughts."

Isaac smiled. "It'll cost you a quarter."

Ruby dug into her pocket and held up a coin. "Settle for a dime."

He took the coin and turned it over in his fingers. "Aubrey told me why she broke up with me all those years ago. Her intent was not to hurt me. She thought I deserved better than her."

"That does make a difference. All I know is that when I see you two together the attraction is clear," said Ruby.

"It was that obvious, huh?"

"Sure." She elbowed him. "I can tell when two people like each other."

Isaac's cheeks warmed. "I'm not sure what to do about it."

"Well, you got a little time to think on that, don't you?" Ruby shrugged. "Of course, I'm hardly the expert on romance. The guy I fell for is a suspect in a double homicide." She frowned.

Isaac was glad she was willing to keep talking about

Eli. Ruby couldn't keep it all bottled inside. "Did you break things off with Eli?"

"Yes, and I was very careful not to let on that we think he might be a suspect. He gave me an easy out. He was always complaining that I spent too much time away from him because our job takes us all over the state. I told him that I needed to focus on my job."

"I know that couldn't have been easy for you," said Isaac.

The light seemed to go out of Ruby's eyes. "I thought I was a pretty good judge of character. I don't know if I will ever trust myself again to give my heart to a man."

"I know I just said it, but don't be so hard on yourself. When you meet the right person—" he touched his heart with his palm "—you'll know it in here." The second after he spoke, he wondered if that was advice he needed to take himself.

"Yeah, I think it would be better for me to just focus on being super cop single lady."

The both laughed.

After they finished their coffees, they walked back to the motel.

Isaac's phone indicated he had a text. His heart beat a little faster when he saw it was from Aubrey.

I'm headed to work today, but Emily is taking a personal day if you want to get our statements. I would like to start my hike up the mountain no later than nine.

Why had he hoped that the message would be personal?

He texted back that he would be at the foundation shortly.

He turned to Ruby. "If you want to talk to Emily, she's still at Aubrey's condo."

"Great, I will head right over there," said Ruby.

He waved goodbye to her after she loaded up Pepper.

"See you later, super cop single lady," said Isaac.

Ruby smiled, but then her expression changed when her phone made a sound that indicated she had a text. She pulled out her phone and read the screen. "It's Peyton, the head trainer for the PNK9. She has a lead that the stolen bloodhound puppies might be in North Cascades National Park. She's going to follow up."

"Good, I hope that lead pans out. Stay in touch," said Isaac.

He loaded Freddy into the K-9 vehicle and drove toward the foundation. He wondered if he should take the advice he'd given Ruby and apply it to himself. Did he know in his heart that Aubrey was the only one for him? He had a feeling it was going to be the longest drive of his life.

Aubrey placed her gear into her backpack and checked the clock: 8:40. There was a part of her that hoped Isaac would be delayed in getting to the foundation. She'd start her hike and some other member of the team could take her statement some other time.

She wouldn't have to face Isaac, look into his eyes and wonder why he wouldn't say he'd forgiven her for what she'd done ten years ago. That's really all it took, forgiveness.

Aubrey zipped up her backpack and heard a voice behind her.

"Hey," said Isaac.

She turned to face him. Though his expression suggested a sort of veiled professionalism, his blue eyes drew her in. "Hey. I'll be glad to get the final bit of paperwork done over all this, so I can get back to work."

He held up his laptop. "The four of us pieced together the report, so the list of questions we have to ask you and Emily would be minimal."

She pulled her office chair out and sat down, pointing to another chair for him. He went through the questions fairly quickly and closed his laptop.

She grabbed her backpack. "I've got a long hike ahead of me."

"I'll walk you out."

"That would be nice. I'd like to say goodbye to Freddy." She turned to look at him. "Since this is goodbye, right?"

Though the look on his face grew pensive, Isaac did not give an answer. Instead, he simply headed toward the door.

Once they were in the parking lot, Isaac opened the back door of the kennel.

Aubrey reached in and petted Freddy. "I'm going to miss you, little guy. Protector of damsels in distress."

"You were never a damsel in distress, Aubrey. I think that is what I loved about you."

She turned and met Isaac's gaze. "Loved about me, past tense."

"What we called love ten years ago is different from what we have now."

"What are you saying?"

"I love you, Aubrey, the person you are right now." He leaned his head toward her.

Aubrey was having a hard time processing what he was saying. "What about your work?"

"I see how important your research is to you. I like Officers Nielson and Lansbury. Maybe the park police could use some help from an officer and his K-9 partner." He stepped closer to her and took her hands in his. "Look, Aubrey. I'm not sure what our life will be like. I just know I want to be with you."

That Isaac was willing to give the two of them together a shot meant he had worked past his fear of being hurt. He was risking so much by proposing they give love another chance. "We have to start with a clean slate. Do you forgive me for breaking up with you like I did?"

"Yes, I forgive you. And I know your motives were pure. What my mother did was not right, but she didn't really know you or understand what we felt for each other."

She reached up and touched his face where there was a five-o'clock shadow. The intensity of the last few days had not given Isaac much time to shave. "I'm willing to give it a shot. A do-over. Whatever you want to call it."

"Me too." He leaned in and kissed her. "I love the idea of working in the park. The only thing I would love more is if we could do it as man and wife."

Joy sprang up inside her. "Are you saying you want to marry me?"

"Yes, and this is not an immature eighteen-year-old who's fallen head over heels. This is a mature twenty-eight-year-old who knows exactly what he wants, and I want you to be my wife. Will you marry me?"

"Yes, Isaac, I will. Here's to us making a life together."

"I can't wait," said Isaac, gathering her into his arms and kissing her.

* * * * *

Don't miss Ruby's story, Cold Case Revenge, *and the rest of the Pacific Northwest K-9 Unit series:*

Shielding the Baby
by Laura Scott, April 2023

Scent of Truth
by Valerie Hansen, May 2023

Explosive Trail
by Terri Reed, June 2023

Olympic Mountain Pursuit
by Jodie Bailey, July 2023

Threat Detection
by Sharon Dunn, August 2023

Cold Case Revenge
by Jessica R. Patch, September 2023

Undercover Operation
by Maggie K. Black, October 2023

Snowbound Escape
by Dana Mentink, November 2023

K-9 National Park Defenders
by Katy Lee and Sharee Stover, December 2023

Dear Reader,

I hope you enjoyed taking this exciting and romantic journey with Aubrey and Isaac. From the first time that they meet, one of the things that Aubrey and Isaac have in common is their love for nature. Both of them chose professions where being out in the wilds is part of their job description. Aubrey mentions that she first knew there was a God when she witnessed the power of a volcano. For me, nature in all its forms has been a way to connect to the Creator who made the mountains and flowers and butterflies. Whether it is the stillness of the forest in the morning or through the intensity of a thunderstorm, all of it makes me feel closer to God. To sit by a river, lake or on the beach by the ocean and listen to the symphony and eternal rhythm that only God can create is such a treasure. How about you? What part of nature do you enjoy that makes you understand God in a deeper way?

Blessings,
Sharon Dunn

HARLEQUIN
PLUS

Try the best multimedia
subscription service for romance
readers like you!

Read, Watch and Play.

Experience the easiest way to get
the romance content you crave.

Start your **FREE TRIAL** at
<u>www.harlequinplus.com/freetrial</u>.